UNRAVEL

KATHY COOPMANS

Unravel

© 2019 Kathy Coopmans

Cover Design- Ellie McLove

Editing done by My Brother's Editor

Proofreader- Cat Parisi.

Formatting- HJ Bellus/Small Town Girl Formatting

This is a work of fiction. Names, characters, places, and incidents are products of the author's imagination or are used fictitiously and are not to be construed as real.

Any resemblance to actual events, locales, organizations, or persons, living or dead, is entirely coincidental. All rights reserved.

The unauthorized reproduction or distribution of this copyrighted work is illegal. No part of this book may be used or reproduced electronically or in print without written permission by the author. All rights are reserved.

PROLOGUE

Ellie

Locking the door to my apartment, I slip off the sky-high heels before making my way down the short hallway and enter the bathroom where I turn on the shower and strip myself of the light blue slip dress I'd decided to splurge on. For once when I went out, I wanted to wear something besides jeans to the dance club, to tame my wild hair, to feel beautiful and let go.

And I did.

I felt gorgeous. Like Cinderella the night the Prince finds out who she was.

But, the man who swept me off my feet, he wasn't a prince, he's more like a knight in shiny black armor. Deep and mysterious and intriguing. A man who captures everyone's attention with a single glance.

I knew right from the get-go he'd possess and control me.

And, I let him, despite that gnawing sense of danger in my stomach.

He looked vaguely familiar, but I was too wrapped up by the uncontrollable emotion that spun between us to place him, too off course from the usual way I lived that I became vulnerable and for once in my life, I gave in to the stirring depths of need.

"People say it's hard to find a beautiful woman, but easier to find a pretty one. I wonder what they'd say if I told them I found both in you."

I wanted to tell him he was lying.

I didn't.

Twisting the satiny material in my hands, I bring it to my nose and let out a whimper.

"It smells like him, and much like the sins we committed."

Folding it neatly, I place it on the vanity and step into the shower, the scalding water stinging the marks he left on my skin only hours before as I tilt my head back and reminisce. Then I'm going to secure them in the drawers of my mind, bring them out and dust them off when I'm lonely.

I can't help recalling first how the man ate me up all night with a lusty gleam in his eyes, how my stomach dipped after we danced, and he ran his nose along the side of my neck. How, for the first time in my life, I let myself get lost in the arms of a man.

I should have known better.

"Come home with me," he said.

Those tempting words were all it took for me to say yes.

I shudder from the memory of his mouth as he kissed me dominantly, backing me across a darkened room until my back hit a window. The coolness of it doing nothing to calm the flame of my heated flesh.

I gasped, heart pounding when he slid his hands up my bare legs while his tongue explored my mouth with sensual glides of his velvet tongue.

"Softest skin I've ever felt."

My breath caught, pants escaped the higher his hands went, and the urge to tell him to stop, the part of me that knew what I was doing was reckless and wrong rose from my lungs, but it never escaped my lips. His warm tongue left my mouth and went to my neck, his strong hands grabbed hold of my ass, and lifted, growling when he realized I wasn't wearing any panties. My legs wrapped around his back and my arms around his neck. I wanted him, even if I'd regret it.

He pushed against me, his hard cock long and thick underneath his jeans, and God I wanted to come right there when he eased a hand down the crack of my ass, his fingertips grazing my wet folds.

"Fuck." He growled, stroking me once, twice before plunging a finger inside me.

He used his teeth to pull both straps of my dress down my shoulders, then drew a nipple into his mouth.

I moaned, banging my head against the window as he drew, bit, licked, and fingered me into a frenzy. I ran my hands through his black hair as he scraped his teeth from one breast to the other, his stubble scratching along my flesh, his mouth showing no mercy toward my stiff peaks.

"You are so fucking tight, so fucking wet; I want to devour you."

I couldn't speak.

I just tugged onto his hair a little tighter.

He kissed my neck, and I shivered, everything in my body was lighting on fire.

"I want you; are you sure about this?" I still couldn't speak, so I grabbed his face and answered by sealing my mouth to his.

Removing his finger, he circled slowly around my clit. It was delicious, wicked torture and all I could do was scream and moan from the sensation of his touch, the way he worked my body was so intense that when he placed me back on the floor, stripped me of my dress and himself of his clothes and rolled on a condom, my legs were violently shaking.

"I don't think I can go slow, if I hurt you, please tell me."

I nodded.

He lifted me back up as if I weighed nothing; I wrapped my legs around him once again. He palmed my ass with one hand, slid his cock between my sex with the other and thrust forward, impaling himself fully inside me.

"Oh, holy hell," I uttered, squeezing my eyes closed. The man is just as big down there as he is tall and wide.

"Jesus, are you alright?"

I was, and I wasn't.

I was burning up, my fever rising for him to move, this man was filling and stretching me with deep-seated pain and inexperienced pleasure.

"Yes." I urged him on by arching my back and squeezing his thick pulsating cock.

His lips met my throat as he pulled back and plunged again.

Each push and pull sent me higher, and the stranger, the man whose face I recalled, but his name sat at the tip of my tongue fucked me into oblivion against the window, our heated skin slapping against one another's with every wicked stroke.

My arousal climbed and climbed as he kept hitting the one spot I needed most.

Never in a million years, a thousand romance books, a hundred romantic films, did I think it would feel like this.

Right. It simply felt right.

"Fucking beautiful, you are goddamn perfect — everything a man like me wants and more. If only you could see the way you look, the way you're taking my cock up against this window, the lights behind you. Christ woman, you're an angel that's entered my darkness. Your cunt is so tight and warm." His husky tone, even darker words against my sweaty skin soared me higher.

A quiver ventured through my center, this man intrigued me, held me prisoner by his shade of black.

He bit my collarbone, and I cried out as the pain itself clenched my walls around him, and I came on a ragged and heaving moan.

"That's it, sweetheart, milk it, take what I'm giving you and drain us both dry."

I cried out when he pulled out of me, grabbed my hips and pressed my front to the window, bending me at the waist enough for him to thrust back in.

My hands had nothing to hold onto but the fogged up glass they slid down.

I panted and bucked as he skidded his fingers down my stomach and began circling my clit.

"Please, I need more," I whined, my voice sounding like a child. I didn't care, because whoever this man was, I knew I would never see him again.

I caught his reflection in the glass, his inky black eyes that drew me in earlier like gravity were a little distorted through the fog, but I knew he was a dark fantasy, a dark knight that could never be mine.

His powerful aroma came off of him in waves.

Dangerous and intoxicating.

God, I'd give about anything to remember his name, to let him seep into my veins and take away my pain. To be his dark angel and for him to be the knight to save me.

He brought my mind back when he nipped the lobe of my ear, and I moaned just as he scraped his teeth across the back of my neck.

"I'm close; I need you to come one more time before I carry you to my bed and fuck you again."

He pistoned into me then, his manly grunts giving me

what I needed to come, and when he stilled, I could feel his hot spurts filling the condom, his cock pulsing and throbbing.

When he was done, he pulled out of me, wrapped his arms around me and carried my relaxed body to his bedroom where he fucked me again before tugging me to him and ordering me to sleep.

I didn't, because for some strange reason, my mind cleared and I remembered who he was.

Panic. It struck through my veins.

Loss and grief. My mind screamed it while my heart fought that this man didn't pick me up to toss me back into living in my past.

Nightmares and heartache and emotions I battled hard to make disappear.

I waited until he was sound asleep, slipped on my dress, and stumbled down the long hallway to where I grabbed my heels and clutch where they'd both laid by the front door.

And I left.

And as I rock back and forth on the shower floor, I feel it.

The danger that's coming.

Leaving me nowhere to hide.

CHAPTER 1

Two weeks later
Ellie

"This home is gorgeous. Is Eric's boss moving in or out? I mean, the man who greeted us at the door just flung it open and walked away. We could rob this place blind. Not that we'd have anything to steal," I prod jokingly at my best friend Norah; it's with much less humor than when we walked in a bit ago and my jaw dropped when I noticed how barren of life it is.

No furniture, no paintings on the wall, no television. It's completely empty.

There was one room with a locked wooden door at the far end of the hall upstairs. I'm assuming it's the master bedroom since none of the others appeared to be.

The style is unusual for the Westbank of New Orleans too. It's a remarkable log cabin home you'd generally see settled at the foot of the mountains in Colorado. High vaulted ceilings. Wood beams throughout the entire place. It's rustic and to be able to decorate it would be beyond my wildest dreams.

I let out a trembling sigh, place my hand on the smooth wooden staircase railing and descend the stairs.

"I'm not sure; he owns Behind Closed Doors. I already told you this. Maybe the guy is redecorating. I don't know, ask Eric." There is something in how Norah is quick and to the point, something that sets me off balance in her attitude and it doesn't have to do with the club the man owns. She's lying about something; I can sense it in the air, smell it all over her. The scent is so strong it practically fills my nose.

"Forget it, it's not my business." I wave it off; it's not like I'll be coming back anytime soon anyway.

Eric is a friend of ours we met a few years ago after he moved into the apartment above the coffee shop in our neighborhood. He's a bartender at Behind Closed Doors and working at this party. He said his boss told all his employees they could invite whoever they wanted, which now, after Norah's weird behavior, I'm beginning to wonder if she didn't drag me here to meet a guy.

A guy for her, not me.

Behind Closed Doors isn't just a normal club either; it's a sex club for swingers. It's what Eric calls the whole sexual experience, and here I am standing in the middle of one of the Kingpin's home. A worshipped pimp from my understanding.

I might have recently had a one-night stand with a man I don't know, a man that drudged up the worst memory, but that type of lifestyle scares the ever-loving shit out of me. I would never have sex in front of someone else, let alone multiple partners.

But that's me.

I wave off the weird vibes floating off my best friend, my thoughts drifting to this stunning house.

This home is meant to impress, all open and airy, it's ravishing. There's something about the intricately designed place with high ceilings and impeccable detail that screams dangerous and lonely. Like if you made a tiny gap in the shiny hardwood floor, it would leak story after story that would tinge a beautiful soul with sadness before turning it the blackest of black.

This place reminds me of the happiest and worst days of my life.

Unlike this home that could use some tender loving care, I used to live in a gorgeous decorated house that was bright and lively. It screamed life despite being too big for a family of three.

Until one day it was nothing but cold, damp and empty.

It started the day my mother died at the age of forty-two from early onset Alzheimer's. I was seven. It was less than two years after the diagnosis when her mind surrendered to the disease, and from there on, she declined rapidly. She lost her memory of who I was; it was even harder a year later because when she died, a part of my father died too, the part that made the man care he had a daughter to look after.

It wasn't until I turned twelve when he introduced me to a woman named Elizabeth that I got my tentative father back. Elizabeth and her two children, Whitney, who was the same age as me and her son Shadow, who was two years older, brought life into our house.

After the two of them married, Whitney and I did everything together; she was the sister I never had. And Shadow, after a while, his true colors came out. He was the perfect definition of what his name meant. A dark shape that follows everywhere you go.

I was polite and friendly to him when we were around our parents. The minute we stepped out of their sight, I avoided him at all costs.

He was a constant unwanted observer. A psycho who I knew was trouble. For the sake of my father's happiness, I kept the way he acted at school and the rumors that followed him like the disease he was to myself.

Doing so was the worst mistake I ever made.

Then one day, my life crumbled. Whitney and I came home from school to find reporters surrounding the gates leading to the house, police officers inside, my stepmother sitting stoically and without tears in my father's favorite chair and Shadow sitting smugly by her side.

Grief and sorrow.

They seeped into my veins and clung all over the faces of my family's employees.

And there was absolutely nothing that could have prepared me for the shattering news that came out of the detective's mouth. My father was dead.

He and several business associates died in an explosion on one of his oil rigs. A freak accident that left me an orphan at an early age.

The investigators ruled it accidental. If it wouldn't have been for some of the other men who died, families being satisfied with the ruling, I'd have thought they were murdered, especially after the things that went on the minute the case closed.

It wasn't a few short days later; I overheard Elizabeth talking with Shadow. She went on and on about how in a few short years, Shadow was to leave for training for his birthright next to her brother, and he needed to behave himself until the time came. Elizabeth was the sister of an Irish mobster, and after I heard her, it didn't take long to put two and two together.

I ran to my room and recalled the happenings around our home before my father died. Elizabeth must have persuaded and turned him into a dishonest man; he became involved in some shady business deals with some even shadier people. At the time of the investigation, I didn't quite understand what the detective meant when he'd ask me questions about my father's business.

Elizabeth is nothing but a poisonous black widow who played on my father's grief of never getting over losing my mother.

Things declined from that day forward. I could hear them whispering behind my back. My mother's jewelry disappeared from the safe in my father's office. Shadow became more of a stalker, and the three of them spent money on unnecessary things. Before I knew it, I became an unwanted girl in my own house.

She got rid of everyone and everything that meant anything to me. No more household staff who were like family, because they were all fired. Every single one in a blink of my young girl eye.

My entire life as I knew it stripped away. Elizabeth and her devil children sold everything in an estate sale to the highest bidder and when I screamed and fought and attacked, letting them know how cruel they were. They laughed in my face and let me know my father's oil business was handed over to her family. From there it would be sold. My legacy and the hard work my father put into owning a successful business was gone.

Then Elizabeth shoved me into the system with nothing but my wealthy-known last name. I was all alone and rightfully scared.

The thought of how scared I was makes me want to weep.

Thankfully, after two months of living in foster care, I was saved by our family's cook — the woman who taught my mother and me so much about life. Renita Williamson fumed her way into social services and demanded they place me in her care. It was a quick transfer for Renita to become my guardian due to my age and the fact I knew her.

"Are you sure this dress isn't too short?" I tug down the

hem of my deep purple backless lace dress and loop my hand through Norah's arm, shoving away the weird feeling that things still don't seem right.

I don't know why I care about the way I look, because frankly, I could give a shit what others think about me. Maybe it's the Bentleys, the Maserati's, parked in the driveway. Reminding me of the times evil men would drive up and enter our home as if they owned it.

My father used to tell me not to worry, that everything he was doing was securing a future for me. I believed him because not once had he ever lied to me, not even the times when he came home drunk after my mother died.

No, those nights were when he was the most honest. Crying and telling me how sorry he was that he couldn't find his way back to me.

"Please don't ask me about the dress being short again. If you do, I'm going to rip it off and expose the hottest body I've ever seen on a woman. Also, if it makes you feel better, if I weren't into men, you and I would be married by now, and when people asked what attracted me to you, I'd say have you seen her legs? They are tone and long. How about her ass, you really can bounce a quarter off it, trust me, I've done it, and don't even get me started on her rack, because, cleavage." Norah smiles, her grin full and sly.

"Oh, shut up; you work out as much as me." I slap her hard on the ass.

My heels click on the marble floor as we walk through the empty dining room and into the loggia that overlooks an Olympic sized pool.

My jaw drops. There are at least a dozen red velvet couches, tables with candles, bartenders making drinks, and red drapes that surround what appears to be private little cabanas.

It's an outdoor paradise that screams seduction. I suck in

a breath, feet wobbling, body in confused chaos. If this is a sex party, I'm no longer going to have a best friend, given that; I'll kill her.

Thanks to my overactive mind as a child, a father who loved skeet shooting and taught me, I'm a perfect shot. I'll nail her between her pretty deep brown eyes. Not really, but I'll be angry.

My palms turn damp and sweat beads at the nape of my neck. A peculiar sense that I'd been here before tugs at my awareness, all the while I'm confident I'd remember this place if I had.

Nervously, I straighten my shoulders, swallow, rub the pads of my fingertips against my thighs as we step out into the open. My nerves fray and float away in the wind — apprehension tugging at my temple.

"Norah, what in the ever-loving hell is going on?" I breathe hard through my nose to temper down the angry vibration of my muscles, the rage bubbling in my veins ready to boil any minute.

"I don't know."

She's lying again, and I am pissed.

Women who were laughing a second ago, stop and glare our way, their beady little eyes raking up and down Norah and me in contempt, scowls on their judgmental faces before they turn up their noses, carry on in conversation and sip on champagne in designer dresses and expensive shoes, diamonds and gems draping off their necks and ears.

Bitches. I hate women who act like they are better than others.

Men in expensive suits give us the once-over, and rest their gazes on our breasts, licking their lips and flashing shiny Rolex watches on their wrists before bringing a crystal tumbler to their mouth.

I'm not impressed.

These are the types of people giving me another reminder of why I hate money. Not that I care who they are, or what they do, I don't; it's the way they think they are better than everyone else. The way the men hold back no reserve as their gaze strips me naked.

"Jesus, I need a drink, like a double shot of the good strong stuff," I whisper, suddenly feeling more uncomfortable in my skin.

I take a deep breath. I don't like it here at all.

I narrow my eyes and look around, a deep instinct controlling my body. Someone here is staring at me with intent to harm. Well, whoever they are, they won't see my dread. I've masked it well.

The corners of my mouth draw up slightly into a genuine smile when something catches my eye.

"Wow. Now that is nature's beauty." I'm thankfully drawn from my nerve-racking surroundings as I take in the view beyond the house. Lush green trees decorated in twinkling lights line a walkway leading to a wide open area lined with magnolia trees in cream and white.

I've only seen one other field full of something as beautiful in my life.

I damn near topple onto the ground as a memory arises.

"Come on, Daddy, let's pick Mommy some of our favorite flowers." I ran ahead of him through the field of purple, blue, white, red, and pink blossoms, my ponytail swishing behind me.

"I'll race you, Bluebonnet, last one there is a rotten egg."

I look beyond the field filled with hundreds of blossoming magnolia trees as I absorb some of the best memories of my life and what I see is just as mesmerizing.

I let out a melancholy breath and watch the sunset with an unwavering gaze as the fiery bright orange orb slowly sinks. Threads of light linger and spread across the sky, blending with the rolling clouds, and streaks of red, orange, gold, and blue swirl until all that's left of the sunset is a color palette of dusty light mauves.

It's almost as stunning as a sunset behind Pleasure Pier in Galveston, Texas where I grew up, a place that will forever hold some of the best and worst memories of my life.

But my awe-inspiring view becomes obstructed when a very tall man comes into sight. My breath catches in the back of my throat, and that knowing knowledge of being here in the past kicks me in my teeth, just as a hard magnetic pull unravels through my veins.

Tugging and pulling and making me damn near stagger.

The man approaching us is like a dark silhouette walking straight out of the horizon.

The crowd quiets and everyone parts like the Red Sea.

My eyes slowly crawl upward, long legs, thick muscular thighs hidden underneath a black tailored suit. A crisp white shirt covers what I know are abs made of steel and his sculpted chest and shoulders are all tucked away beneath his matching suit jacket.

I stop breathing when I get to his magnificent face. One filled with scruff I know all too well is softer than it should be, and he is staring directly at me.

He's caught me off guard, and he knows it, judging by the hint of arrogance in his eyes.

Damn it. That's twice in a matter of weeks I've been captured in this man's spell.

The power that swirls around him as he approaches is overwhelming as his bright green eyes take me in like a caress across my skin.

I become lost in the translation of his command.

His head tilts to the side, those eyes wandering fast, up and down my body so penetrating it makes me want to hike up my skirt, jump in the pool and cool off. Or drown him and my deceiving friend I can feel shaking in her skin next to me.

This man holds some terrifying power amongst these people. Well, he's in for a rude awakening because I won't let him know he's dangling it over me.

His mouth, the same one that kissed me everywhere a few weeks ago, twists into an over-confident grin — an invitation welcoming me into his house of sin.

"There you are, I was wondering if you'd make it. Good to see you again, Norah. So we meet again. Hello, Ellie. I'm Logan Mitchell."

No. He can't be.

I'm utterly speechless when I'd love to tell him sarcastically that he is a son of a bitch, but his sultry rough voice glues my tongue to the roof of my mouth.

Damn Norah and Eric for putting me in an unwanted position; I should hate them both for this, Norah, especially.

Logan's nostrils flare, dark eyebrows lifting, and something similar to disgust flashes from the depths of his eyes, his mouth turning down as he twists his muscular body and scans the crowd before rotating once again and locking his green pools on my outraged blues.

I've no idea if people are gawking at us, but by the way his posture went from relaxed to an angry stiffen, I would say yes.

I don't care. Every single one of them can fuck themselves.

An overwhelming surge of heat rushes through me as his gaze lands on my mouth, setting my skin on fire.

He's drawing me in like a sedative. One you need, yet your mind is afraid of what will happen once you are pulled into the dark.

He's the reason why this place feels familiar. Logan Mitchell is the man I went home with, the man who brushed his big hands across every inch of me as if he knew the places on my body to set me aflame. Technically he probably does. Logan is the man whose name I never asked for, the same as he never asked for mine. He blew into my life like a storm — thunder and lightning knocking my sanity into a spool of want and need and consumption.

He's someone I never wanted to see again.

He made me feel in ways I never saw coming. He took the hollowed out woman in me and filled me up with the passion and attention I needed for just one night, and he's Eric's boss? The man just about every woman in New Orleans wants. The man just as many men despise as wish they were him — a man who is paid top dollar to teach women how to please a man.

A glorified male whore.

The only time I've ever gone home with a man, and he's the one. Oh, God. Not only am I embarrassed, I feel absolutely sick to my stomach.

"The one and only Ellie Wynn." Norah breaks up the tension, lets go of me and turns toward Logan. "I'm uh, just going to grab a drink and let Eric know we're here. Usual for you Ellie, Logan would you care for something?"

I nod, unable to form a word. Afraid if I do, it will be answered with my foot up her ass and a palm across Logan's handsome face.

"I'll have a Budweiser; thank you."

Shocking, the man does manners underneath his walls of muscle.

I take Logan in. God, he's beautiful and he's wearing a smug look that says 'I'm the kind of man who gets what I want, and at the moment, it's you.'

Well, screw him, he will not have me ever again. Especially now that I know who he is. But that's not all I know about Logan Mitchell, and by the hard stare he's giving me, it's clear he knows it too.

Bastard. Liar and deceiving pig.

Tonight, he's much different from the jean-wearing man I met. But it's him — the very man who I've thought about many times. The man who has had me losing sleep at night because I'm scared right out of my skin — the man who has me wanting to burn a hole by telling him off right through my tongue.

I hate him.

I want him.

I'm scared of him.

My heart clatters against my ribcage and my panicky breathing speeds to dangerous levels. I suddenly feel light-headed, and my mouth is ignoring my brain's instructions to at least acknowledge the man. I stare while he stares back at me. Those forest green eyes are overflowing with something like admiration.

They spear right through me in a way I don't want them to. Bursting with confidence, with a softness, and if I'm not mistaken, a little bit of worry.

"Welcome to my home. It's good to see you again."

For him, maybe. Not for me.

"Even though it's empty and reminds me of a dark dank awaiting tomb, it's lovely." I found my voice. It's sarcastic and rightfully so.

His muscular chest shakes with light laughter, and shit, what a chest it is. Big and rumbling with strength.

"You've got a quick mouth on you, Ellie. I like it. It makes me wonder what else it can do." The intensity grows in his eyes while his words hit me between my thighs.

Throbbing.

The night he brought me here, he melted my panties.

Tonight, no matter how much he tries charming me, they won't be coming off.

"You'll never know."

"We both know I will."

No, he will not.

"Speaking of having a quick mouth. Here's something you can chew on and swallow. I won't submit to anyone. If I want you, I'll have you. If I don't, I won't. You, you're a…" Shit. I can't even force the word, and I refuse to bend to his patronization. Him trying, pours more gasoline to the raging fire burning within.

"A male whore? Is that what you're trying to say? I was one, Ellie. I haven't been in almost a year."

Possessiveness surges. Hard and heavy that it consumes my mind. I want to punch every woman he's had before me. It's a crazy notion when I don't even know this man.

Logan takes hold of my hand that's dangling at my side and drops a kiss across each of my knuckles, dancing eyes searching mine. His touch is soft, familiar, intimate, and my skin tingles where his lips graze.

"I sense there's more your gorgeous mouth would like to say to me. Perhaps go to hell? Fuck off? Maybe what the hell is going on? Why was I at a dance club the night I brought you here and had the best sex of my life when I could have been at my club? Would you like to know what I'd like to say to you?" He reaches up and strokes my cheek.

No, I really wouldn't. The man already has my mind traveling back in time. Right back to ten years ago.

"I'd like to tell you to get on your hands and knees, to spread those sweet thighs, pull my hair when I bury my tongue in between them. I'd like to know if our night together was as good for you as it was for me. I love to tell you to scream; only this time saying my name when I make you come."

I roll my eyes and swallow, pressing my thighs together as memories of him asking me to do all but the last assault me in the spot his intention wanted to hit.

Logan Mitchell, I knew the name, but on him, I like it— Bossy, sexy, overly confident, dangerous. Most importantly, he's one of Shadow's friends.

My stomach curdles, and bile churns.

I also can't help the way my tongue betrays me by unhurriedly darting out and running across my bottom lip, instead of telling him whatever game he's playing is pissing me off. My body wants to thrust me forward to taste his lips, while my rational brain jerks me back in. Being reckless again isn't going to keep me safe.

"You might not be anymore, that doesn't mean what you did was right. I'm curious, how many people would I have to perform this sex act on, in front of or, would you be between my legs while another man was thrusting himself inside my mouth? Maybe, I'd be the student you'd put in the middle of the class and bend over your desk."

Steam. I see it rolling off him and within seconds anger charges in the air.

I keep right on pushing because my peace of mind has to know if the one man who destroyed me is here.

"Where's Shadow? Is he going to emerge the same as you?" The mere idea of anyone, regardless if they're a snob or not admiring that piece of shit the way they did Logan is enough to split me in two.

I shake my head, my fury and disgust rotting my insides.

"Here you two go."

I jerk my hand from his, accept my drink from Norah, feeling the uneasiness in her stare where it rests on the side of my face. Ignoring them both, I turn toward the pool, rather rudely, letting them carry on while I toss back my tequila, and brace a hand on the couch in front of me. Tuning

UNRAVEL

them out entirely and examining my shoes. Suddenly feeling so far out of my comfort zone, I let out a silent scream.

More so for falling into bed with a stranger when I knew. God, I knew I'd seen his face before. After I showered the night I left here, I wanted to pack my bags and run, knowing my past had caught up with me. I may have never spoken to Logan before, but I remember him sitting in the passenger seat of Shadow's car several times while I stood in front of the big picture window after I moved in with Renita. Unintimidated and glaring as my stalker ex-stepbrother tried to frighten me.

Logan picked me up knowing who I was, he's up to something, and I won't let him become aware of my fear.

A gasp rips from my mouth, and my racing pulse hits dangerous speeds when two large hands cage me in — the oxygen-depleting from my lungs.

I look down at those hands, big and strong, and lose reason when Logan presses up against me. His erection thick and long. Warmth hitting the flesh on my back, a sense of security as he cocoons me in. I had my own hands exploring every inch of his body, every dip and valley of his firm muscular stomach and shoulders. And his cock, my God, how I wanted to run my tongue up the length of it.

I need to get the hell out of here before I lose my sanity.

"I'm sorry. If you want me on my hands and knees begging for forgiveness, then I'll do it. You don't know me, Ellie, but I'll tell you, I'm not used to women speaking to me like that. Your spitfire temper turns me on. For your peace of mind, Shadow isn't here." His lips graze my ear, hot breath causing me to shiver in excitement and fear.

I'm sure he doesn't. They probably drop to his feet and chant out 'what can we do to please you, oh mighty one?'

I slip from his grasp, attempting to regain my composure before I turn around and face him. The last thing I need for him to see is how my mind is tossing me right back into my past.

Shit, I never should have turned around.

Logan is gorgeous. He's also the wrong man for me. Yet, everything about the way he looks at me with adoration feels oh, so right. Like our paths were meant to cross.

"Right. As if I'd ever believe a word you say."

He goes to kneel and my jaw drops.

"Stop." I laugh when there is nothing to laugh about.

Emotions throw themselves into the mix as Logan closes the space between us.

Fear. Lust. Anger. Confusion.

"God, that laugh, such a beautiful sound. Whether you believe me or not, I had no idea you would be at the bar the night I brought you home with me. I asked Norah and Eric not to say anything about this being my party because they knew as much as I did, you wouldn't have come. She went to talk to Eric. I wanted to see you again. I want to take you out. Spend time with you. Get to know each other. You can't deny what we had was more than just physical. And, the only man you'll be performing for will be me, if another man touches or sees what's underneath this dress, I will hunt him down, slice off his balls and force him to shove them down his throat before I cut off every finger and shove them up his ass."

His lips press a kiss to the back of my head, sending tingles rushing as he breathes me in.

"You remind me of my flowers. Free and beautiful and resilient. I might be a dominant man, Ellie. However, it's not by wrapping a collar around your neck and tugging you behind me. I'd prefer to have you walk with your gorgeous head high by my side."

My mind whirls in confusion and chaos while my heart

rate picks up and forgotten dreams of belonging to someone and them to me hit me from his last sentence.

I can't let Logan seduce me. He'd shatter me. Wreck me and mutilate those dreams the second he decided I wasn't enough to keep him from wanting other women.

"You're wrong; I'm not any of those things, and you don't know me well enough to tell me who I allow to touch me. I won't be going anywhere with you, as in ever. Don't try and manipulate me; I'm not a fool, Logan. You knew who I was and you played me. Please, if you haven't told Shadow where I am, I beg you, please don't." I pant, my lungs trying to gulp in the air that suddenly becomes too thin. This is too deep, too profound, too damn confusing. Most of all, it's hurting me in ways only others that went through what I did can understand.

Devastation. It threatens to wreck me all over again.

"Never. I'm not a spy for Shadow. You have my word on that. You don't know me well enough to find out just what I'll do if someone touches you, but I want you too. You aren't a fool. You're the most beautiful, sassy, sophisticated woman I've seen and I want to know every little thing about you. You're a survivor."

"No. You and I don't mix." He's a whore for shit's sake. One the police turn a blind eye to.

Logan Mitchell is trouble.

"Wrong, Ellie. We do, and that's what has your panties in a twist. That is if you're wearing any. Should I check?" He surveys me and smirks as my face flares with a heated flush.

"You're a real asshole; you know that?"

"Yeah, sweetheart, I do. I'm finally seeing the woman that left my bed without a goodbye. When I realized you left, I couldn't go back to sleep, I laid there and thought of your beautiful face and figured you must have caught on to who I was. I can't stop thinking of the way you screamed when I fucked you. The way you had no idea how rich I am and even if you did, you would have wanted me for me and not the things you thought I'd give you. You haven't left my mind. I'd kind of like to spend time with you, and by time, I don't mean picking you up off the ground after you passed out from not breathing. Although, giving you mouth to mouth wouldn't be a problem. Breathe, Ellie."

I should be chock full of disgust at him and me. Instead, my mind follows along with imagining his mouth on mine again. His body on top of me or to sit out here amongst the flowers and trees and just talk.

"Please, don't. What we did was something I've never done before. I want you to leave me alone."

Humorous laughter rolls from him as he runs a finger up my spine and grips the back of my neck.

My entire body shivers in ecstasy.

"Somehow, I find that last sentence to be a lie. I get why you wouldn't believe a word I'm saying. I'm not that man anymore. Please, can we meet and talk? Give me a chance to explain. You want me, don't deny it. I bet if I stuck my hands between your legs, you'd coat my fingers with the juices from your sweet pussy."

God, he's an arrogant, dirty mouth, irresistible asshole. A bad, bad man through and through.

And one-hundred percent right.

"If I weren't positive one of your friends or many fuck toys here wouldn't stuff me full of bullets before the sting hit my palm, I'd slap you. A friend of Shadow's is no friend of mine." My heart rocks in fear, and I detest it, hate that Logan has this kind of influence over me to draw it out. God, I want to kick my ass for going home with him.

Never again will I be so stupid and drawn toward a man's seductive words, a masculine face and a body packed with muscles.

"We aren't going to discuss who I fuck unless I'm fucking you."

"What?" I teeter on my feet, crossing my arms over my chest — stupid move. Logan's eyes divert down to my breasts. My nipples harden under his darken stare.

"You are an overconfident prick." I need to calm down before I get right in this man's face and cause a scene.

That's the thing though about being bitter after life dealt you a shitty hand, you tend to not put up with shit from anyone. At least I don't.

"I'm that and more. I've done terrible things, and I'll continue, it's in my blood. One thing I'm not is a man like Shadow."

"And you expect me to believe you? Fat-fucking chance."

A blow of terror and knowledge and self-destruction shoot through my veins. It's obvious he knows what Shadow did to me.

I feel sick and used. It pelts on me with the force of a hail storm. I'm in no way prepared to talk about it with him. Possibly never.

"I'll take that chance and prove you wrong, sweetheart. I'll let you go, for now. I'm going to get to know you. I'm going to have you again and again. Next time I'm going to fuck you until you scream my name. I'm a man who always gets what he wants and make no mistake, Ellie; I want you."

Shudders multiply, spreading fire down my spine, shivers scatter, winding me up and up until my body heats and flames.

"You're either lying or hiding something from me. I'm not the woman I used to be. I lost my entire world. I've been trampled on, and brutally raped. A violation to not only my body, my mind too, and if you think you can take me on a ride and drop me off where nightmares live, then you underestimate me. Tell Shadow, Whitney, and Elizabeth if they come near me I will make them pay for what they did to my father and me."

A blanket of guilt covers Logan whole. The man is full of blame.

God, I need to stop being a bitch and give this man the benefit of the doubt. It's so hard when I'm scared.

"Elizabeth is dead. She died about five years ago. I'd prefer not to discuss Shadow in public, you are safe from him, Ellie. I give you my word on that."

Safe? I haven't truly felt it in years, but for some unexplained reason, I believe Logan. Still, my fear will get the best of me until Shadow takes his last breath.

I attempt to regain my composure and scan the crowd when I want to bend forward in hysterics over Elizabeth, over Logan, over the irony that has tilted my world upside down and left me dangling in thin air.

A choked laugh catches in my throat. Dreams really do come true, at least partially. I don't need to know how the witch died, as long as she's dead. "Good, that means she's rotting in hell. The only way I'll ever be safe from the man is if he's rotting next to his mother."

I take several breaths, trying to get it together while Logan stands completely still. His bottle of beer hanging from the tips of his fingers.

I'm crazy to wish he'd drop that bottle and take me in his arms. To whisper over and over the promises I'm safe. To let it sink in.

"He isn't dead. He isn't in New Orleans either. Listen, Ellie. I'm sorry I scared you. Please, can we go talk? I don't want you leaving here with a fist full of worry."

The last is so much easier said than done.

A woman catches my eye, looking at Logan like he hangs the moon, and me as the woman who just strolled in to cause a scene. I'd like to thank her for momentarily pulling my mind back together. To remind me that I don't know Logan. He could be lying as far as I know.

"A woman is glaring at me; she better not be your wife or girlfriend."

I'd ask the Devil to take my soul if she is.

"Whoever it is, it's neither. I don't have a wife or girlfriend."

I wait for him to turn around and see who I'm talking about, it doesn't come. Probably because he can feel all of them at his back, it's hard not to.

"I don't know what you want with me. I mean, look at these people, then look at me. I'm not like them."

I don't bother looking at him. I can feel his displeasure and anger at my words leak right out of him.

Confusion and madness and mayhem twirl my brain like a spinning top.

This is all just too much.

"No Ellie, you're not and that's what makes you so damn perfect. I won't stop coming after you. I don't think I'll ever stop."

I'm swimming in a river full of shock to speak anymore. I hold my pose, my heart slamming like a ping-pong ball in my chest.

Anxiety and panic. They are wretched things, and they overpower me.

"I'm sorry. Every time Shadow and I pulled away from your house, I told myself it was the last time I'd go, but then I thought about what he might do if I didn't tag along. A part of me has blamed myself for what he did. I don't underestimate you; I admire you."

God, who is this man standing before me with anguish dripping from his every word? I swear I can physically feel his guilt and hear his pain. It's gnawing at the noise in my head.

Horrid memories try pushing in. I block them out; I can't talk about what happened to me, not in front of people who would likely laugh at me, dropping to my knees.

"What happened to me isn't your fault."

"No, it wasn't, but I knew how out of his head Shadow was for you."

I've never had a one-night stand until Logan. I've never been with a man in my life. Not willingly anyway, and as I watch him walk away, leaving me with piles of questions and head in the direction of the gray stoned guest house, I'm scared agreeing to that night is going to ruin the strong and independent woman I am.

On second thought, it already has.

CHAPTER 2

Logan

"The fuck is wrong with you, Logan? Ellie was all Shadow talked about for as long as we've known him. You couldn't stop at fucking her, could you? You had to go and invite her to your party? When Shadow finds out, he's going to lose his shit. Not that I care if it drives him crazier than he is, it's her safety that concerns me. For many reasons. I heard people were glaring at her like they wanted to strike her down and the party ended less than twelve hours ago. Imagine how many others know."

Lane, one of my two younger brothers, starts in on my ass with a long-winded hurl of worries when he comes through the door of our office. His tone, obviously full of rage. We haven't spoken much since the day of the party. He'd left shortly before the first guest arrived. Guess he's pissed.

That makes two of us.

I keep my mouth shut, I know my brother, and he isn't done. Probably shouldn't have told him I slept with her. The thing is, we don't keep secrets from each other. Learned a long time ago how secrets and lies can ruin a man, and here I'm holding back from telling Ellie one.

Pretty goddamn pathetic.

"You've fixated on her for years. I told you to make her yours a long time ago and not build on our fortune. Why wait until now when things could blow up in our faces? I swear to God, I won't let you ruin that woman. Ellie has been through enough. Either you start explaining, or I'll tell her everything."

One of his questions is easy to answer. I won't be saying it out loud. I knew one taste of Ellie's sweet little body would be too much for even a man like me to handle. Wet and tight and fucking delicious.

Mine.

And I want to fuck her again in every position possible.

"Which one of your concerns would you like me to address first?" I keep my dick from growing, and my anger in check. Lane keeps it up and brother or not; we'll be going at it with our fists.

I'm aware I shouldn't have extended an invite to Ellie, but I was going out of my mind not seeing her again. When I'm around her, I feel peace. No obligations, no pretenses. No bullshit.

Total peace.

Ellie handled herself with dignity and grace at my party, while the women acted like jealous peasants out to destroy. Every woman I felt stabbing me in the back with their possessiveness as I made my appearance known. As if they had the right. They were looking at Ellie like they wanted to spike her in the eyes with their heels. And the men looked at her like they wanted to fuck her, and she isn't one to be touched, talked to, or shared. Can't blame the men because the woman is as beautiful as she is laid back. The men know the rules and would never lay a finger on her. Now a few women, in particular, I'm not so sure about. Something tells me Ellie would handle them just fine. Still, I wouldn't want anyone from my past anywhere near her, let alone trying to hurt her.

I'll make them aware if they even look her way, there will be hell to pay.

Fuck, do I want to mark her as my territory. Own her. Possess and control. I will break through her tough built up exterior. It's a goddamn challenge I accept.

In the meantime, I might not own the people I opened my house to, but my brothers and I control them, and if one of them steps across the line and touches her or opens their mouth about a secret I have yet to tell Ellie before I do, I won't hesitate to ruin them.

I make very few exceptions in my life. I've murdered, came home and washed off the blood and slept like a baby. Women, on the other hand, not sure if I have it in me to physically hurt one. I know someone who does, and I'd see to it they are put in their place.

"My biggest concern is Shadow. He'll be out of prison in less than six months. Early release on good behavior, as you know. That held him off from kidnapping Ellie years ago as he planned. He's going to find her and what do you suppose he'll do when he finds out about you?"

Think he forgets the minute I get word he's out, I'm gunning the raping son of a bitch down, and until I do, Ellie will be surrounded by an army of protection.

"I hope he does. All the more fun I'll have when I kill him." Shadow is a crazy man; no emotion except anger and his bloodthirstiness for Ellie run through his screwed up mind. I've waited a long time to put him six feet under for what he did to her. I'd like him to suffer before I slice his throat, knowing that gorgeous woman is mine.

He blamed me for ratting on him, for turning him in. I

don't snitch. That's not my style, but I know who did, and so does Lane. If someone crosses me; I go after them in the brutalist of ways. Simple as that. Some I torture until I decide they've had enough. Others get a bullet right away. Whitney and Shadow deserve to suffer for going after Ellie, and so did their dead mother. Unfortunately, I wasn't the lucky one to kill her. That privilege went to someone else.

"Right. You have it all planned out, don't you? How about when Whitney decides to blackmail us with our client list? Politicians. Doctors. Lawyers. Celebrities. We have some very influential people who trust us, Logan. We pay big money to keep the law off our ass. I suppose you have that all figured out too. Those people get exposed and we are as good as dead. Swear to God, your head is so far up your ass that you forget where your loyalties lay."

My fingers immediately flex into fists. I don't need to defend my loyalty, Lane of all people knows it, but my reply is one he'd best swallow down with his words. "You better watch it. I'm as loyal as you are. Whitney knows better than to turn my laptop over to anyone." Somehow, about a month ago, Whitney slithered through security at the club and stole my laptop that could ruin a lot of people if she gets someone to hack into it. That happens, and we'll be rolling in deep shit. The problem is, she took it and vanished. We've been looking for her since. It won't be long before she's found. I do not doubt that at all.

I have information on the bitch. She breathes a word and she's as good as dead.

As far as our safety? We're fine. Greed is a crazy bitch. Toss a few grand to crooked cops and they have your back. Just like every other greedy man and woman out there wanting a piece of the Mitchells, they know there's more coming if they do their job.

UNRAVEL

As I watch my brother pace toward the bar and pour himself several fingers of scotch, my mind drifts back to Ellie.

The first time I saw her in person, was when she stood in front of her window and glared at Shadow. He and I met when we were kids when his uncle brought him over one night. His uncle and our father were good friends. The man ruled with as many morals as he could with being a mafia king, unlike his nephew who pulled the wool over everyone's eyes. I didn't know shit back then about the life I was born into, the connections my father had, but I recall how the old man was always trying to tame Shadow's psychotic mother until he gave up and let her fend for herself. Putting his focus on Shadow instead.

Back then, Ellie used to rile Shadow up bad. The irrational ass went out of his head not seeing her after he graduated from high school and moved to New York to start training with his Uncle. Every opportunity Shadow got, he wanted to fly down and see her, kept on about Ellie being his. I thought he was crazy for it, but for Ellie's sake, I'd talk Shadow into flying to see me, then we'd make the eight-hour drive from here together.

Then the time came for me to take over our business. I worked my fingers to the bone, had other things going on and worrying about someone else was one thing I didn't have time to do. I had no idea he raped her until sometime later, and it gutted me. I didn't have any idea about Whitney's involvement at the time either. It rots my gut every time I think about it.

Therefore, I sought justice the only way I knew how.

To watch Shadow fail and take Whitney down.

Shadow always talked about ruling the underworld with prostitution. I guided him, taught him what I'd taught myself, and in the end, his greed took over, making him plenty of enemies. Within a few years, he went from riches to rags.

He deserved it — power tripping fucker and disgrace to humanity piece of shit that he is.

Whitney? She's simmering in her pot of shit. Stewing and if she thinks stealing from me is her way of retaliation, then she's in for the shock of her life.

There hasn't been a day where remorse hasn't gnawed me to the bone. I think that's why I stayed clear of Ellie. Of course, I always knew where she was, protecting her from afar, but I never approached her.

I'd never spoken a word to her before seeing her at a club a few weeks ago, and for some reason, she left an impact on me years ago and an even bigger one on me after I fucked her.

Ellie Wynn is for a good reason, reserved. But she's also self-assured, fascinating and the most fuckable woman I've seen. For years I thought about sinking between her legs, kissing her everywhere and tasting her pussy, grabbing that tight ass, marking her there and fucking her until she couldn't think straight.

That's not all. For the first time in my life, after one night with very few words spoken, I want to sit down and converse with a woman about anything and everything, and it should scare the shit out of me. For some unexplained reason, it doesn't.

I've always thought she was beautiful, thick mane of black hair, sky blue eyes, curvy and as naturally beautiful as any woman I've seen, and after the other night, her sassy mouth makes her far more exciting than I'd expected.

The woman speaks with elegance, a side order of smartass, and her mouth gets me hard. She's the only woman who I've ever allowed to tell me off and my dick tapped against the zipper of my pants watching her hold that fight not to lash out even more.

I wouldn't change a thing about her.

Fucking beautiful. An elegant uncommon white swan in the middle of a life full of black.

All the women I had before her bent over backward for me, shoving away other men the second I snapped my fingers. They allowed me to fuck them in front of strangers, share their bodies with other men and women in hopes they'd snag me. They do the same for my brothers — every one of them wanting to be the one to claim a Mitchell. To tame and get us to settle down.

Not Ellie though. She might give a shit about the life I lead but, my money, my power, they don't mean a thing to her, and I find that sexier than any woman who will drop and wrap their mouth around my dick.

The beauty lost everything, and still, there is something about her strength that shines like some brilliant bright guiding light.

The kind you see from afar, drawing you in out of curiosity to watch it glow, a magnificence, unlike anything I've seen in the purest form. A strong woman full of life and innocence you can't find anywhere else except in rarity.

That's what she is, rare.

Scarce and unusual in a world full of sin and corruption. A society built on it, like mine.

One glimpse of her up close a few weeks ago almost brought me to my knees. Eyes that shined like stars, drawing you to explore the spinning sadness in their indigo blue depths. The black of her pupil surrounded by a ring of loneliness.

At one glance, her eyes tell an entire story.

Heartbreak, the missing of love, the pain of deceit, and

the flame of an inner force that would never give up no matter how many times she was beaten down.

And fuck all if she wasn't beaten down by a couple of deceiving women and a scumbag who did her dirty and wrong.

Since bringing her home with me, I've categorized every move she makes, grouping them in my mind.

Strong. Independent and unbreakable.

Stubborn.

I don't want to break her; I want to bend and please her.

Ellie doesn't just wear her emotions on her sleeve; they flow from her like a refreshing stream in the middle of a desert.

So fucking sweet I want to dip in and taint. Dirty up only for me.

I want inside that tight, little body every chance I can get.

One touch of her hand in mine, her body pressed close, those lips painted in sheer gloss, I knew I had to have her. I had to get a morsel of a taste before I swooped in and caught her in my web of lies, and it angers me that wanting her is driving me out of my goddamn mind.

I hardly know the woman, and I might have grown up living a fucked up life, but years ago when I heard Shadow did what I feared he would, it pushed me over the edge, tugging a conscience I didn't even know I had. The things he and his sister did to that woman are worse than everything I've ever done, and I've done some low and mortifying things, but to rape and destroy and bully an innocent woman.

Fucking never.

Not only did Ellie brutally and inhumanely lose her innocence, but she also lost her mother, and then her father. Her home, family business. Her life. All because of a woman who corrupted Ellie's father. Glad the bitch was shot in the back of the skull by a man who caught onto her before she got her claws into him.

Is Ellie unaware of a lot of things? Yes. Harmless? Not a chance. Especially to a man like me. One without a soul.

Lane tips back the last of his scotch and places his tumbler on my desk, hands attached to a body made up of more loyalty than any man I know. He grips me by the back of the neck, pulling me toward him. Green eyes just like mine giving me a look he's given me my whole life. The one that says I got your back, always will, but if something happens to Ellie, you'll be on your own.

He's one of the few who has ever been able to calm me down and damn it if I haven't needed a lifetime of calming, especially after living years in the farthest depths of hell — all flames of fire singeing and scorching my skin.

I screwed up the minute I saw Ellie the night I fucked her, which wasn't part of our plan. Couldn't help myself. I was shocked stupid when I saw her. The woman has a body to worship and fuck. Long shapely legs, dainty and delicate fingers, arms toned and leading up to the most creative elegant neck I've ever wanted to bite into, straight hair flowing down her back and begging for me to fist and pull and mess it up while directing her toward my straining cock.

My brother and I look each other in the eye, the worry seeping from him like a leaky faucet.

"What you should do, is leave her be."

I know I should. We both know I won't.

"Yeah, well, that's never going to happen. I want Ellie; what the hell is wrong with that?"

Telling lies, hurting a woman who doesn't belong in our world is what's wrong. The thing is, I'm obsessed with her, and I know there's going to come a time when the truth will come out about things I've done. Even so, there's no reason why I can't pursue until I figure out how to keep her.

"Jesus man, do you hear yourself? What's wrong is *you*, brother. Is she worth letting go of the lifestyle you live, because I'm here to tell you, that woman might be strong, and the night you spent with her might have brought out something you didn't expect was inside you. However, there's not a chance in this lifetime she'll continue with you once she finds out all your secrets. Let's not forget the women who will make a mission out of destroying her."

He's right.

If Lane thinks I'm going to feel guilty about it, he's wrong.

Ellie unknowingly has me plotting out a way to keep her when I know I can't. It's making me agitated. Has my muscles twitching. Fury and resentment have been coursing through my veins ever since I touched her.

All of it toward me.

I can't stop myself. At this point, I'm not sure I want to. Not when Ellie is sizzling in my blood.

"Ellie knows who I used to be. It doesn't matter if she's worth it or not, you and I know I won't give her up. End of subject, Lane."

He releases his hold, shakes his head and strides back toward the bar, pouring himself another drink.

"You might not teach anymore, but you still participate in the fun. Notice how you didn't say you'd give it up? I sure did. Do you honestly think she's the type to have a threesome with you? How about watching you fuck another woman in front of her? How about you watching another man fuck her? You're an asshole, man. So far out of reach. Sitting over there saying you won't give her up when you don't even have her. You shouldn't have started any of this with her. We've followed in the footsteps of our parents. Dad groomed Mom to be like him, to live in his world and in case you've forgotten, she became addicted to strange men's cocks after he died. Those cocks led to drugs and some shady ass shit. Life became a hundred times worse for you after Dad died. It fucked Mom up because deep down it wasn't for her, she did it for him. You better think again if I'll let you prime Ellie to be like our mother. I won't stand by and watch an innocent woman get reeled in, then let go and drown."

The fuck is his winded self going on about?

The muscles in my forearms tighten. The thought of anyone touching Ellie but me is enough to make me want to start pulling the trigger.

"You talk like I'd force a woman to do something she didn't want. I won't share Ellie with anyone. You're standing there acting like you're ashamed of what we do. As far as Mom is concerned, she hated me from the day I was born." Jesus, he pisses me off. We've shared many women; he isn't any different than I am when it comes to fucking.

"No one will have access to Ellie but me. At least not in the way you're talking. I don't want anyone else, Lane. Fuck, you think I want her anywhere near our club? And I will have her, thanks for the vote of confidence, brother. Thanks for being on my side. Thanks for trying to help me figure out what to do." Shit, this is the first time my past makes me ashamed when it shouldn't.

"That's not what I meant, and you know it. I'm not the one placing a woman in danger from every direction. Listen to me, damn it; you think those women wanted to hurt her the other night, you wait. You don't have it in you to be faithful to her, Logan. Admit it." He takes a breather and runs his hands down his face. "I loved everything about fucking who I wanted when I wanted as much as you. I haven't been mixing business with pleasure in years. That all changed when I first held the person I love a hell of a lot more than some random lay. Have you forgotten the hell I went through to keep? Jesus, I can't even finish that sentence."

He doesn't know what the hell he's talking about. Any man who would cheat on Ellie is a goddamn idiot.

"I'll never forget what you went through, Lane." The night he can't talk about is burned in his brain as well as mine and our younger brother Seth's.

That love Lane found to keep his ass out of our clubs is in the form of his almost five-year-old daughter, Lexi Mae. The kid is the best thing to come into our lives. The light in our life. Blonde curly hair, a unique personality, always dressing in pink and asking questions.

My brother is the best father I know. The man will probably have some heartbreaking love story just waiting to be written, one where a woman saves a broken man instead of the other way around. He deserves happiness, and so does Lexi. So does our younger brother Seth, and me.

I lean back in my chair, a lump growing in my throat, can't stand the thought of Ellie looking at me with disgust now that she knows. She doesn't have a clue as to the mark I've left on women.

"They go near her, and they'll regret it." I'll stop at nothing to keep Ellie and those she loves safe. Even if I die trying.

I haven't been able to get that woman out of my fucking head since I fucked her. The one my cock gets hard for at all hours of the day and night.

Son of a bitch. I have big problems when it comes to the darker side of my life as well as the ones arising with Shadow.

Spinning around, I gaze out at the magnolias that were here when I bought the place a few months ago. They remind me of Ellie, beautiful and full of life, a life that could quickly be snuffed out by the darkness my storm is about to create.

Leaving them bent, broken, and the beautiful petals falling to the ground before they have a chance to bloom.

At what point I decided to become addicted to something I never wanted to kick until I spent one night with Ellie beats the hell out of me. Our father died before we were old enough to decide on whether we wanted to be a part of his world.

I could have become hooked when our mother got involved with a man named Angelo shortly after our father died. The prick always showed up at our house in his big black Cadillac and called her every bad name you could think of before they'd head out for the night. It could have been when she'd stumble in drunk several hours later with a different guy or two. At times she'd bring home women, and they'd tumble into her bedroom, leaving us to listen to grunts and moans while we sat holding our younger brother Seth while he slept. Every damn time we covered his ears so he wouldn't wake up and ask where she was.

The times he wasn't asleep, and he'd cling to her leg, she'd send her lover down the hall, and he'd threaten to beat Lane if we wouldn't take care of what she called, 'her little problem.' I always stood in the way and let them strike me while Lane consoled Seth who only wanted attention from a bitch who loved no one but herself.

Our mother's wrath, her hatred toward me, I was used to it. There wasn't a chance I was letting her touch Lane. I might be an asshole, but I love my brother, and I'd take her fists any day if it meant she never abused him.

Could have been when I did everything she told me to do, and it still wasn't enough for her to stop beating the shit out of me and convincing me at a young age her idea of how I could make millions. Always reminding if I wanted to stay with my brothers, and eventually, the three of us become what we were born to be, I would do what she said, or she'd kick me out. Bitch was so whacked, the business would have gone under if it wasn't for a family friend doing us right.

Or, it sadly could have been the night our mother decided she didn't have a damn thing left to live for anymore and blew her brains out in her bed while we slept in our rooms down the hall.

Didn't bother Lane or me one bit she was gone, but Seth, he loved her in spite of the bitch not giving three fucks she had kids who needed the loving touch of a mother. Not one who filled their heads with learning the oldest profession known to man.

To use our bodies and become whores. To teach women how to fuck.

Christ, I hated that woman with everything in me.

I give him a stern look. There's so much more to the lives of the Mitchell family than people know. All the things that went on behind our closed doors while growing up would make a priest give up trying to save us.

But, Ellie, she could be the one to pull me out of something I've enjoyed far too long.

"You need to protect Ellie, let her know everything you've done and then leave her be. That means now. Don't go barging in her life, sweeping her off her feet and having her fall for you without telling her your secret. You know better than to blindside someone. You do, and you aren't the man I thought you were."

Yeah, well, unfortunately, I'm not the man he thinks I am. Luck dropped in my lap. I'm holding onto it and making Ellie mine. Leaving me the honored man who gets to pound into her pussy, watch her back arch when she comes, to see her spread those thighs, to watch her lips separate when she drops to her knees — all the delicious wicked things I want to do to her.

"Shit," I mutter as he doesn't say anything more and walks out the door. I need a drink and to purge on whiskey instead of thinking of Ellie as my chaser.

But that awareness, and want and need, they don't subside.

It doesn't matter how much I drink; it won't erase her from my mind.

This new addiction I have is going to be a sweet tortuous ride.

CHAPTER 3

Ellie

"Come on, Ellie; you're the one who went home with him and here you are angry with me? Unbelievable. You wouldn't speak to me on the drive home, and you still refuse to talk to me. I told you when we left Logan's place; he isn't married. He doesn't have a girlfriend, so what's the big deal? It's not as if you haven't already slept with him. Talk to me. He's asked Eric twice for your number. I'm going to give it to him if you don't talk to me."

The big deal? Oh, I could rattle off a half dozen of big deals and Norah will still try to get to the detonator button to set me off.

Push and explode.

I smash my eyes closed against the swell of potency that is Logan Mitchell. It hasn't left me since I walked out of his door. The man is so powerful, so influential; he's taking up all the space in my mind, and it terrifies me that he's there. I've allowed him to place a crack in my walls. It won't be long before the big brute of a man tries smashing them to smithereens.

Blowing out an aggravated sigh, I finish the window display I've been piecing together between customers most of the day. Our little consignment shop called Ebony and Ivory doesn't make us wealthy, but it pays the bills and gives me the necessities I need to live.

I'm proud of our store, and I believe my parents would be too. It puts a smile on my face when a single mother walks in here with her kids, and they walk out with bigger ones on their cute faces. Carrying bags full of clothes, shoes, and accessories they couldn't afford anywhere else.

"It's not the clothes, the hair, the jewelry or any expensive thing you wear. It's the way you carry yourself underneath that makes up you. Hold your head high, push your shoulders back and show the world you matter. If you always remember that, Ellie, whatever you do will be successful."

My mother told me that every time we went shopping. At the time, I didn't understand. Now it's the motto Norah and I painted above the awning outside.

"I slept with *him*, not him and others. Logan owns a sex club, Norah. How many women do you think he's slept with since me, before me? God, don't answer that. Let me absorb this, and maybe I'll forgive you, it's just going to take a while to forget you betrayed me." I suck in a breath, shame sliding in with it.

Norah is the last person in the world I thought would let me down and that hurts more than her deceiving me.

"The last thing I need is to get involved with a man like Logan Mitchell. I will not be with a man who wants other women. I am not made that way, Norah, and you know it."

It doesn't matter how good-looking or sexy he is. How he told me he didn't teach anymore, how energy races through my skin when he's near, how I love the way he draws some primal need out of me with his dirty talk. He's hazardous. But damn can the man take me to a place called paradise.

Pleasure-seeking intoxication.

Even though I have nothing but a nightmare to compare Logan to, I'm sure the way he screwed me until I was coming over and over is from all the women he slept with before me. It's not that he's more experienced, hell, everyone is. It's how he went about getting it that bothers me. I have every right to feel the way I do. And in finding that out lowers my self-esteem below existence.

Makes me angry at myself how I didn't pay attention to my surroundings when I followed Logan to his home the night we met. If I had, that familiar feeling of being there would have slapped me upside the head like a two-ton brick. I would have bolted out the door and never looked back.

Logan is all dark and broody and mysterious. The kind of man who could easily convince you to jump in the sack with him with one little twitch of his talented mouth.

It's frightening how I can still feel him everywhere too. Skin tingling as if those eyes were roaming over my body, his big hands following behind. Making me scream and shudder and shake. The man turns me on and scares me. It's a puzzling feeling two differing emotions at the same time.

Makes me want to pull my hair out.

"You don't know what Logan's done since that night, Ellie. Have you talked to Eric yet? He feels awful. I can tell you he said Logan doesn't come out of his office since the night you went home with him, and newsflash, my friend; you weren't raised to judge people either."

Guilt anchors down my throat, and I'm instantly drowning in it. She's right, I wasn't.

"I talked to Eric this morning. We're fine. I'm not judging anyone. You should have told me, Norah. I couldn't care less if he lives there. Let me give you a piece of old news. Do you remember the guy who would sit in the car with Shadow across the street? Logan, he's that guy, Norah."

Now that my shock has worn off and Logan isn't all up in my space with his apologies and addictive smell, those soul-sucking eyes and the intensity between us. The intoxicating lust and hostility swirling around, my hardness has returned, and Norah is the one getting the brunt of it. I'm not the type to let someone toy with my life or my feelings. I did enough of that with the danger I have a feeling is about to tilt my world again.

It doesn't matter what Logan said about him not being like Shadow, I don't trust him, and after this, the man would need a damn good explanation for me ever to consider it.

"What? Are you sure? Did he bring it up? I mean, what did he say? Where's Shadow now? Whitney and Elizabeth?" It's her turn to be shocked. She stares at me, her mouth parted, eyes slightly bugging.

It's what he didn't say that has me this close to becoming an unsteady mess.

I'm overwhelmed with the need to know what he's up to. To let him take and give what I need because there's something about him that makes me want to feel, but that's my choice to make — not his, and not Norah's. Not anyone's.

A tremor crawls through my being. A distinctive one that if Logan were to walk through our door right now, he'd draw me toward him, a prisoner held captive, edging toward the cliff and falling toward all of his carved, molded rock solid muscles. God, I've never wanted to lick and feel and watch a man's body unravel under my tongue in all my life.

Quite comical when I've never given a blow job or had willing sex until him in my twenty-eight years.

He left me with a night to remember, and that's the way it should stay.

"Yes, I'm sure, and if you tell your mother before I do, I will never speak to you again. I'm not sure where Shadow and Whitney are, Logan told me Elizabeth is dead though.

Don't give Logan my number either. I'm not angry, Norah, I'm hurt. If you can't see how wrong it was to blindside me like that, then you're the one with a problem." God, I don't want to discuss this anymore. If only I could be lucky enough that the information I've given her would stun her mute, then I wouldn't have to.

"Logan faults himself for what Shadow did to me. At least that's what he said." I've never in my life felt another person's guilt before, but then again, the man has me twisted all up, I don't know what to believe. Truth or lie? I'm not sure. It makes everything about him much more confusing and questionable.

Gritting my teeth, I make my way around her and head to the back of the store, grabbing the pile of designer jeans I priced this morning. Right now I want to finish the day and go upstairs, lock myself away for a little while, down a couple of shots and think, but I know that's not going to happen, so I brace myself for whatever it is Norah has to say.

"Wow. At least one of them is rotting in hell. Logan's guilt goes to show he isn't out to hurt you, Ellie. If he wanted to, don't you think he would have by now? Logan is the first man you've ever shown an interest to, as in ever. Sure you've dated, but you weren't the one watching the two of you the night you met him. I was. He made you smile; he made you feel good about yourself. He couldn't take his eyes off you. I saw it, and excuse the hell out of me if I want my best friend to be happy. Those women who looked at us like we were nothing are jealous of you, and they have a right to be. You are beautiful Ellie. I won't say I'm sorry when I'm not."

Norah knows I couldn't care less what others think of me, and yet I did. I let those women get to me, and I allowed one night with a man bust me wide open.

There are a hundred things I want to say right now about those women. If I open that stinky can of worms, we will end up being here all night. Upper class once debutante snobs who would scream bloody murder if they got their precious hands dirty. Yeah, I know their kind — socialites who think themselves above everyone else when they have more skeletons in their closet than most people. The majority probably haven't worked an honest day in their lives unless you count lying flat on your back with your legs wide open.

Not that women who choose to stay home aren't hard workers. I've no doubt most are. These women though, they are unlike any I've seen, including ones on those reality television shows.

I see the kind of man Logan is too, the man hiding behind a wall of secrets, and like a stupid woman, he's going to suck me into his winded vortex and leave me breathless. If I let him devour my body again, I can see myself wanting more, and something strikes me dead center, screaming loud Logan Mitchell is about to bring my past into my life.

Very capable of killing me.

A shiver of fear, a warning whispers in my ear from a night that changed my life forever, it crawls like little insects all over me as it bites and burns.

My entire being shakes, and I drop the jeans all over the floor. My chest tightens as I press my hands to my head and fall to my knees.

Unwrapping my arms from around my stomach, I shook my head, lifted my dress and ran when a man I did my best to avoid, climbed out of a muscle car that pulled up alongside the curb, asking if I wanted to have a good time.

Fear sprinted at the devious chuckle rumbling out of his disgusting mouth.

"Fuck off, Shadow," I'd said. "You and your sister are nothing but pond scum. Bottom feeders who use people. What should I expect when you were brought up by a woman who uses men to work her way to the top."

Up until the creep graduated high-school, he provoked and cornered me, always thrusting his erection into my backside, grabbing and shadowing me. He would follow me and pin me with stares that if I allowed, would have had me running. The guy is a lunatic.

"At least I have a mother to raise me. Have to say though, every time I see you, you blossom more. Wonder how that hole between your legs would open for me?"

I folded my arms across my chest as if they'd hold in the cries and heartache and fear from the viciousness of his words.

"You are sick. You better leave me alone, or when I get home, I'm going in, grabbing my gun and shooting your pencil dick off."

Malicious laughter rang. Loud and disturbing.

The asshole comes around once or so a month and sits outside our house. Always when I'm home by myself.

I hate him and want him dead.

"After tonight, I won't be sitting outside your little shoebox house anymore. I have a kingdom to make larger. Get in the car, Ellie. I've been waiting a long time to fuck you, to tie you up and make you mine. I'll show you just how big my dick is."

Panic clawed at my chest.

I took off in a sprint when suddenly his car slammed to a halt, and heavy footsteps hit the sidewalk behind me. My arms and legs were burning as I rounded the corner just a half block from home. I let out a scream, hollering and begging for help when he caught me, and we tumbled to the ground with him landing on top of me, muffling my whimpers with his dirty grabby hands. He dragged me to his car, tossed me in the trunk and drove to an abandoned parking lot a few blocks over where he yanked me out by my hair and threw me onto the ground.

I fought with all I had, but Shadow overpowered me. I went still when he flipped me onto my stomach and ripped my dress and panties.

"I've been waiting a long time for you to become legal. Let's see if little miss perfect is still a virgin. My sister claims you are."

"No. Get off me." I tried pulling his hair, clawing wherever my hands could reach, trying to escape what I knew was going to happen. To not be a victim and not let Shadow take what's mine to give, but when he gagged me with something, tied my hands behind my back and unzipped his pants, I knew there was no escape.

"Not happening. You smell like purity. One of these days I'm going to lock you away and keep you forever. No man will touch this beautiful skin after me. I'll leave my mark again and again. My uncle died, and I'm going to run our empire. Once I get things in order, I'm coming for you. I need a queen, and I choose you. I hate to hurt you this way, hate seeing you cry, but I promised Whitney I'd draw blood."

I haven't seen Shadow since the day he walked free. For years I had eyes in the back of my head, always looking over my shoulder. It wasn't until a few years ago when I finally stopped having nightmares, and now I'm afraid to close my eyes.

That day two mentally unstable people who hated me as much as I hated them twisted the screw in my life as far as it could go — wrenching until it stripped.

That was the last and most valuable piece of me that they stole. If I ever see Shadow and Whitney again, I will kill them where they stand.

Before that, Whitney didn't leave me alone. No, she was out to destroy me. That girl tried making my high school years a stark raving madness of hell. Every smile that lit up her features was the wrong kind. It was fake. Like she ran on the cold nastiness I knew she had instead of any form of genuine affection, and not just toward me, she directed it toward anyone who lived on the wrong side of Galveston County.

People were afraid of her. I wasn't one of them.

To her, I became the trash she trampled on with her shoes. Shoes bought with my father's money, and her friends followed. I did my best to ignore her, kill her with kindness, until one day I had enough of being bullied by the little bitch who took a shit daily the same as the rest of us. I turned the tables and beat the ever loving crap out of Whitney. I would have pounded her face into the ground and left her for dead if Norah hadn't pulled me off her.

I think back then, if I weren't so out of my head with trying to wrap around what happened to me, I would have blown heads off and dragged bodies behind my tiny Ford Escort through the streets of Dallas. Renita almost landed in jail when the District Attorney called to tell us Shadow's charges were dropped due to it being his word against mine. The crooked snake had a rap sheet already, and still, they wouldn't prosecute.

I'm no fool; I knew they were paid off by Elizabeth. It's all part of the twisted underground corrupted game.

Blood money.

Anyone who puts greed before doing right by someone can never be trusted. I learned that and much more from my father who loved his green, but not once did he put it before my mother and me. And, after what Elizabeth did just for money, I despise it with every fiber of my being, and no one will convince me to have more than necessary.

"I know enough about Logan to know he isn't my type," I tell her as I frantically scoop up the jeans in a hurry and walk back out keeping my head down while I start refolding and placing the sizes in order the way I had them before.

Norah might have done me wrong, but if she knew that horrible night escaped the box slammed tight in my skull, we'd never get out of here.

Damn it.

I wish I could erase the man from my mind. Logan is like

a god that could quite possibly be the death of me. Literally. I need to get answers and then shake him from my thoughts before the memory of him tangles me up.

"You don't know that. Logan could be what you need. He brought you out of your shell when no man before him could. Are you afraid because of what happened?"

My head shoots up, and I give her a don't-you-dare bring it up look.

Lord knows it's already dangling on the edge of me. Once I let go, I'll be slipping into a hole I may never climb out of.

"Please, this has nothing to do with my past." It does though really. Everything in my personal life has revolved around the worst night of my life.

It frightens me how fate has dropped someone from there in my lap and here I am wanting to find out why when every part of me is telling me to stay away.

My throat burns to scream, a setback weighing heavy on my shoulders — eyes stinging with both anger and tears. I won't cry over what happened, not ever again. As much as my mind pleads to fall into grief, my heart protests, telling me I'm strong when Shadow, Whitney, and their ice-queen mother tried to leave me broken and weak.

I glare at Norah; she isn't going to back away from this. I know her, she's like a loose cannon when she wants something, ready to fire and nail you right between the eyes.

"Ellie, I can't begin to imagine what it was like for you, but I was there, remember? I saw how you lost yourself, stood by and watched you fight to gain back your strength and inner beauty. I held your hand, went to therapy with you. God, this isn't about me; it's about you. It's about me sitting back and watching a woman who has missed out on finding true love, of being consumed by the best feeling in the world — a man's touch. Going home with him was an ice-breaker for you. You had sex. I'm sure it was incredible mind-blowing, stimulating sex. I can't just let it go. Please, for yourself, try to look at the positives in Logan rather than the negatives in him and your pasts. Open your beautiful soul, Ellie, and while you're at it, you could share a bit of how good the sex was."

The sex was everything I needed and nothing I expected. It was wild, untamed, wicked and for one night I let go.

I want to do it again.

"I don't want to talk about it anymore. Drop it, or I'll never forgive you."

She stares at me as if she doesn't know me. "Why not?"

"Because I said so. I get what you're saying, but by opening my heart, I'll be making myself susceptible to getting hurt." Or dead. I'm afraid having it broken by a man like Logan is something one would never recover from. "There's also the fact; I will never be a woman of flash and flare. I will never link myself with the rich, especially his type."

"I don't buy for one second those women are truly his type — first stage clingers is what they are. Maybe you should get to know the man before you cast a stone."

Maybe she should shut her mouth and let me make decisions on my own.

The way Logan stood there like he wanted to tell those people off breaks into my mind. His apology. The way he looked contrite and devastated. The way he disappeared and never came back the entire time we were there. Which was all of a half hour because I felt eyes on me everywhere. Not to mention the woman I thought might be Logan's wife or girlfriend kept glaring at me like she wanted to rip my hair clean from my scalp and claw my eyes out. Eric ended up telling me she's Logan's secretary. The woman glared at me the same way the handful of other women there did, all of them doing their best to shuck me full with intimidation. It dripped off them like poison.

I wanted to slap it off every one of their faces and spit in their eyes.

As confused as I am, I still have the urge to want to be near him. Logan has a captivating pull, one that without difficulty draws you into his world. Rough and smooth. Rugged and abrasive with his dirty words and caring with his hands.

That practiced, hooked seduction he wears easily made me feel something I never felt in my life. Made me consider being wicked and adventurous. Things I've never thought about doing in bed. Like jump in with my body first, head and heart last into the muddy waters of need.

I saw those same things in the way women looked at him as if they'd drop to their knees and submit.

I don't want to be the kind of woman who is helpless to his magnetic power, weak and in desperate need of a man to take care of her. I need a man to hook me the old-fashioned way — by my mind, body, and soul.

Then again, I have a feeling that's what Logan wants. He's chosen to start with my body first.

Exhaling, I wonder, am I as thick skinned as I think I am, because I'm not just physically attracted to Logan. I'm enchanted. Drawn in by the darkness he alludes, caught up in his charm, enticed by the way my body reacted the minute I saw him again, and overly curious as to why I can't get the man out of my head.

It's maddening.

"I understand Logan scares you, and there is nothing wrong with being scared. Don't let that man slip through your fingers without giving him the chance to prove the type of guy he is. If you don't like him after a date or two, then you don't. Logan is captivated with you, and you need to live.

You were spontaneous the night you went home with him. Be that way again. Here, Eric gave me this. It's Logan's business card." She shrugs, hands me the card, and takes the jeans from my hands, placing them in the empty cubby. Her way of telling me this conversation is over.

I'm glad. I need a breather from it all.

Tears gather in my eyes. God, how I wish it could be easy to forget what happened to me, to dream big. To let Logan consume me and me him. I just don't know if I can ever trust the man.

I want to. God, do I ever.

My eyes drop to the black card in my hand. Gold letters form Logan's name. Above it reads Mitchell Brothers Holdings, below is an office as well as a cell number.

"How many brothers does Logan have?" Eric told us Logan had brothers, how many I never asked.

"Two. Logan is the oldest. Lane is the middle, and then Seth. Their parents passed away. I'm not sure how. All I know is their father started the club. They grew the business from there."

I bet they did by selling their bodies.

Sadness blisters my heart. I know all too well how Logan and his brothers feel if they were close to their parents. It's a loss never to be filled again — a hole the size of Colorado right in the middle of your chest.

Jealousy suddenly sits hot in my stomach, its smoke thickening and climbing until it twines around my throat in hostile waves. I force the visions of Logan having women at his beck and call all over the place out of my head.

I take a moment to catch my breath.

Logan Mitchell will never give me what I desire in a man.

Faithful and true to only me.

CHAPTER 4

Logan

"This is bullshit, Morgan, and you know it. Take care of it, or the consequences will be costly."

My blood turns scalding in my veins where I sit at my desk in our office above the club. Unlike the office connected to my bedroom, this one is the last place I want to be. "Don't make me have to come down there. I swear to God the repercussions will cost more than the money my family pays you. As in your wife will be a widow." The warning violence I want to unleash on my lawyer is in my words when I'd like to use my fists and bash in his face.

I better be his top priority, or hell will rain down on his ass. In the form of a bullet for every day he's stupidly fucked me in my ass.

"Just hurry up and figure it the hell out, Morgan and do it like yesterday." I toss my cell on my desk and rub my hands down my face — unresolved anger developing in my chest.

Swear to Christ if he doesn't do his job right this time, I'll blow his brains out along with the people who are dumb enough to cross me.

I sit back, demanding my mind to stay focused, to keep the aggression from taking control of my soon-to-be ex-lawyer's haunting words.

Fury boils my blood; I'm so pissed off I could kill someone.

I clench my jaw, grinding my teeth and gripping hold of the edge of my desk. Angry at my lawyer and sitting around like some pathetic fucker who hoped for a little luck that the woman I want might call me.

The longer the day drags with Ellie ignoring the message to call me on the card attached to the flowers I had delivered to her, the more irritated I become.

The woman has to be going out of her mind with worry. Stupid ass that I am should have never let her leave without telling her Shadow was in prison. She knows I'm dangerous too, and having anything to do with me would put her right back where she doesn't want to be, in the line of Shadow.

Goddamn it.

It's all kinds of messed up too when I could head downstairs in a few hours and have my pick of any woman I wanted. I could teach them, train them and take a few into a room and fuck them, and the woman I want likely doesn't want a thing to do with me. Her smart ass remark about who I am; the things I've done is all the more reason to prove to her how much I've changed.

Can't say I blame her though. My reputation speaks for itself.

Smart woman.

What she doesn't know is she's safer with me because he'll come for her no matter where she is, or who she's with. Man, woman, child, he won't give a second thought of snatching her.

As if my brother Seth could read my mind, he glances my way.

"Having second thoughts about fucking Ellie? Maybe you should go downstairs when we open and fuck someone new. Strange pussy ought to get her out of your system."

Fucking someone else is the last thing I want to do. Not when I'm fuming mad over a long-legged woman with a rebelling mouth on her. One I'd love nothing more than to stuff it full of my cock.

I've been bored with meaningless sex for a long time. It wouldn't be with Ellie. It would mean something and as unreasonable and unexplainable as it sounds, the one night with her did.

"Far from second thoughts. It's guilt from not telling her who I was in every aspect — remorse and sickness for not coming clean about Shadow. I walked away because she looked like she was about to pass out." I'm not the type of man to feel guilty; when it comes to Ellie, I suffocate from it.

I won't approach his other comment because he knows damn well how tempting and easy it would be to wander the bottom floor in search of one or more women. Especially on a Friday night where curious newbies pay top dollar to see if joining our club is something they want. I've been doing this long enough to know which ones are willing, the ones who want to give it a try but are still too scared and the ones who won't ever come back. Those who want it are eager to please the minute they realize propositioning someone for sex not only takes place, it's the name of the game. They'll drop panties quicker than it takes a man to get hard.

Behind Closed Doors has three floors. The bottom is our sex club where swingers and singles meet. The middle is where our female and male escorts play and teach, and the top is where just about anything goes.

"You're preaching to the choir when it comes to guilt, Logan." He scoffs, it's far too knowing. The guy lives daily drenched in it when we both know he shouldn't.

I took care of him because he's my blood, and what happened that caused him to slip farther into the hole wasn't his fault either. Still, it's like beating a dead horse when it comes to reasoning with his stubborn ass.

Since my talk with Lane, I've fought through the many amounts of emotions I feel toward Ellie. Everything about her has repeatedly assaulted the cavity inside my chest, fraying my every nerve worse than all the years she's unknowingly clawed her way under my skin.

I haven't been able to concentrate. Haven't been able to figure out a way to tell her a secret about me that would surely crumble her world, and it doesn't have a thing to do with this place or anything about it.

Once she finds out, she'll never look at me the way she did that night. So full of want and need and passion it burned through my blood. That's if I can get her to talk to me at all. Get her past the fact I betrayed her about who I am.

"I don't know Ellie, from what I do know, I tend to believe she'll forgive you soon enough for deceiving her, it's what she doesn't know, Logan. That's a big secret you hold. We told you to come clean with her, and go after her a long time ago."

True, they did, and the minute I saw her, I deceived her in more ways than one.

As selfish and fucked up as it is, I'm going to do whatever it takes to wedge myself deep into her. To make her feel like she can't live without me. To make her want to need me.

Being inside of her, feeling her arms around me, having her touch me was the only time sex meant a damn thing to me, and I fucked it all to hell by not being honest.

Control.

I need to rein that shit in and remember who I am. A man who goes after what he wants. And in one night, Ellie Wynn has managed to make me feel like I was losing and gaining it at the same damn time.

I have a lot of hurdles to jump over. None of them will be easy. Being a determined man is the only thing I have going until I figure everything out.

"I won't tell you to back off like Lane. You want her; then you need to figure out a way to fight for her once you tell her, Logan. Not many people would have done what you did for Lane and me. If Ellie's who you want, you need to prove yourself to her. Stay the hell out of here when we're open. Focus on you for once and what you want instead of what you and others expect. Go after fate and a woman who, given time, might be the one for you. And, fuck worrying about what Shadow thinks, he's a dead man walking in a prison cell right now. You have my support one-hundred percent."

I shake my head — a smirk cresting my mouth. My baby brother is sitting over there all smug and shit trying to crawl up in my head.

Fuck, I love him.

"Is this some sudden turnaround, a big intervention on your part? I never thought I'd see the day when my little brother would be telling me to give up something he loves as much as me." Seth isn't one to give a shit about much of anything except family, pussy, and alcohol. Family, he can't live without, the pussy, Seth can have all he wants as long as he's safe, the liquor needs to be tamed before he winds up killing himself.

I guess that's part of life, the three of us were handed down a genetic predisposition — our parents' addictive personalities. None of us stood a chance. But Seth, he took the brunt of it with his guilt, and he doesn't give a fuck he's falling apart right before his blinded eyes. Lane and I have tried getting him help. He refuses.

"You have a chance for something good, man. Something

better than random fucks, women wanting you for what you can give them and not for who you are. For you giving rather than taking. You didn't screw up; just went about it wrong."

I lift a brow and clench my teeth.

"Shit, you bump your head or something?" I chuckle, it's the first time in days it isn't full of irritation.

"No, just helping you out is all. We all deserve something good, and Ellie could be your good." He sighs, grips hold of his hair like he does when he's fighting off the beast living inside. At twenty-six, Seth has been through some rough times.

"Now there's something you should be preaching to yourself. You deserve some good, Seth. I appreciate what you're doing; we both know there is no helping the destruction that's sure to come." A burn snakes beneath my skin, leaving me one less wire from detonating.

"Yeah, well, we aren't talking about me at the moment. When the storm hits, you won't be alone to clean it up. Time, Logan. Don't waste it. You have to grip hold of it and fight that bitch."

He would know, his downfall started when he lost his good. The thing was, that wasn't Seth's fault either.

I wonder though what life would be like having her to myself, coming home every night to a home with her in it — living normal, getting something beneficial and feeling all that good in my hands — righting all my wrongs. I'm just unsure how it's possible when some of the things I've done revolve around Ellie.

Brutal. It clenches a fist so goddamn tight, making it harder to breathe.

"I need to take off for a day or two. I need your help." I don't ask for much and Seth would go in my place if I asked. The thing is, I need to fly to Atlanta. That city is the root of some of Seth's guilt. Besides that, this is my deal, and I need to deal with something that's been sitting on the back burner since I got word Shadow would soon be released. I won't ask Lane, in doing so it pulls him away from Lexi. "I need you to keep tabs on Ellie just in case some bitch gets a wild hair up her ass. That means no drinking, Seth." Keeping an eye on her gives me peace of mind.

Seth leans back in his chair, an irritated huff slipping from his mouth. "I might get shit-faced but not once have I done something stupid. I'll keep an eye on Ellie, brother. You have my word."

My baby brother might be a drunk, but he's right, not once has he gotten behind the wheel after drinking. No, it's usually me who picks his ass up. He's not once let me down when it comes to having my back. Same as Lane. Same as I'd do for both of them.

"I'm trusting you. Are you sure?"

Sweat gathers at my nape. What I need to do is go to Ellie and drop to my knees like I should have done and tell her the truth. But as I sit here with a fire burning within me, opening my mouth and spilling my secrets to her when I'm unleveled would hurt any chance of me proving to her that I want more with her. I want to dip and explore. Seek out her mind. Give her more of that pleasure only I can give her. Watch her unravel from my mouth, my cock, my hands, my tongue.

I've never wanted anything more in my life.

The fact I even want to, goes to show how one night can change a man.

It's insane.

"I know how important she is to you, Logan. Just make sure you tell Maggie. That bitch will be over my shit if you don't."

Right. Maggie. The woman who enjoys the perks of working for us a little too much. Should have gotten rid of her a long time ago. The problem is, she's damn good at keeping things running smoothly around here.

Besides that, she's one of the few people who knows all my secrets.

"She might be our secretary; she doesn't need to be aware of my every move. I'm out of here. Call if you need me."

I push out of my leather chair, and head for the door, not bothering to look back.

I need to go to Ellie and make her listen to me, spill my sins at the feet of a goddess, and that's what Ellie is. The kind of woman whose natural beauty draws you in regardless of a past that pulled her under. One look and you never want to turn away.

"Son of a bitch," I mumble. I make my way out of the building, climb on my bike, secure my helmet, kick up the stand, and let her rip and rumble as I ride down the street toward God knows where.

My thoughts consumed with *Ellie*.

So many times over the years, I wanted to introduce myself to her. To get to know her thoughts and rely on hope to make her understand that the things I've done, I would have never done if she was mine.

My mind clicks through our night together, the way she reacted to me—her tongue intertwining with mine, her sweet moans, the way she pulled my hair — all the signs I expected from the woman who needed to be set free — a tempting angel who needs to be teased, worshipped and pleased.

Foreplay at it's best, and fuck do I want to play.

CHAPTER 5

Ellie

The dark clouds are ragged with edges, and the wind begins to pick up. A good ol' unpredictable summer Louisiana storm is coming. The weather here can be brutally humid and rainy in the morning, a storm in the afternoon and turn around and rain again in the evening. It's also a great time of year to people watch as this city is always moving.

Growing up in Texas, I was used to the dry heat, so I took advantage of being outside as much as I could. Like now at seven in the evening where it's stifling hot as I sit in the same spot I've occupied hundreds of times.

The little coffee shop a few buildings down from our store is one of my favorite places to sit and watch people. They have the best sweet tea, most courteous employees and coffee in a variety of flavors and concoctions; I still don't have a favorite.

The street is alive with people coming out for one of the many festivals this city holds. I love living here. After Shadow's charges were dropped, Renita, Norah, and I wanted a new beginning. We settled in the city with many nicknames. Most widely used is 'The Big Easy' which originated from anyone's guess.

It also holds a lot of illicit danger, and by that, I mean the vultures who bring their illegal activity to the streets. I'd be wise to remember that with all that's running through my head.

This time of year is the beginning of hurricane season too, such as the one that's hovering over me sending chills up and down my spine.

Tonight, instead of enjoying watching families sightsee, I'm googling the man who swore he'd someday come back for me, and I'm coming up empty-handed. I can't find a thing on Shadow. Strange or not, I wouldn't know where to look as searching to dig up my past isn't something I ever thought I'd do.

Emotions. I can't turn them down, can't temper them the way I used to no matter how much I wish I could. So many of them are unraveling those double lines of stitching I can no longer hold together.

Horror and pain.

I'm stewing with concern.

It's enough to drive me completely insane.

I'm on edge, slipping and slipping and slipping.

I'm being ripped apart — seam by seam.

I am frightened for my life, and I might not be if I would have let Logan tell me. If I wouldn't be so stubborn and call him.

I'm a damn mess.

Shadow could be amongst any of the people walking by, anytime, anywhere, and I wouldn't see him until it was too late, but I'll never forget what he looks like if I did. Never forget the way his hands felt like knives cutting and slashing me deeply.

A twinge of grief crashes into my mind, this bitter uproar that suddenly limits the flow of air to my lungs. I will never get back what Shadow stole from me. The memories of it are too much. He took the only piece of me besides my heart that was mine to give.

Pain, it rocks right through me, my anger that I didn't let Logan explain not far behind.

I blink out of my daze, steady my hands on the wooden table and look up at the darkening sky.

I won't let Shadow rule me. Not anymore. I've come too far, fought too hard to allow my worries to destroy me.

"Thanks for helping me find what I needed to know about my worst nightmare," I say sarcastically to my laptop, close it, shift to place it in my bag and secure it around my shoulder in case the storm hits and I need to make a run for home. I slouch in my chair, stretch my legs on the wooden one across from me and contemplate whether I should call Logan or not.

The beast of a man has left me with no choice.

"Allow me to help you out with the information. He's an asshole like you said. Owes someone an apology as well as an explanation, rarely takes a woman on a date and has taken the most beautiful woman he has ever seen for granted."

Part of me stiffens at the gruffness in those words whispered by Logan in my ear, while another part wants to look him up just to see what I'd find.

The chair my feet were propped up on slides out, my feet fall to the ground, and Logan slips into the chair, pulling himself close enough for him to rest his hand on my thigh.

A tremble moves through me.

"What are you doing here, and what makes you think I was looking you up? Are you afraid of what I'll see? Photos of you with women? Perhaps having dinner with bad people like yourself?"

My voice is barely a whisper; it's also croaky and thick with quick arousal. Logan looks incredible, and I'm suddenly shifting in my seat.

The flexing of his biceps swallows my focus under the tightness of his shirt. He's far too sexy at the moment for me to be angry.

I drink him in, which is a mistake, his looks only making me thirsty.

Hunger—this untamed lust that smoldered since the moment I laid eyes on him ignites through me like a flame, winding my stomach and throbbing between my legs — increasing my fears and supplying a needy desire.

Typical white dress shirt unbuttoned at the collar outlines his muscular frame. His dark hair swept away from his face. Aviator glasses are concealing his eyes, and there are frown lines across his forehead as well as one tipping down those full lips of his.

And here I sit in cut-off jean shorts with a giant rip below the pocket, a man's wife-beater shirt, and barefoot.

Opposites. They do attract.

He smells like all man, with a hint of mischief and a whole lot of experience. A bait that will snag you in and drive your imagination wild.

I know firsthand just how good he is, and it scares me to death that I want more.

Logan is too enticing for a woman like me who knows she's way out of her league with a man like him. But I want to be tempted, and for some reason, I don't understand, just being in Logan's space makes me feel the safest I've felt in years. I want to crawl onto his lap and let him wrap those big arms around me and hold me close with his strong hands. It's a puzzle with many missing pieces. A mind-bending riddle that I'd love to solve.

But I won't.

Inexperienced, I am. Naïve? Not anymore. Plus, there's something larger than this attraction that any living creature with a pulse could feel it.

"You'll find nothing on me. I pay people to keep my life private. Do I have dangerous friends? You bet your sweet little ass I do. I came by because I had to see you. The way we left things wasn't fair to you. I'm sorry."

For crying out loud, the man is hard to read. One minute he's full of pure raw seduction, the next he's spilling out words that should offend, and now he's snuck up on me with compassion and concern.

"I'm sorry too; I was caught off guard. I don't want to talk about Shadow here."

"You don't owe me an apology, Ellie. I should have told you from the start. I don't want to talk about Shadow here, either. I'd prefer not to talk about him at all."

"I do owe you one. I should have asked your name. I shouldn't have judged you for your way of living. I just…"

Logan pulls off his sunglasses, places them on the table in front of him, and moves ever so slowly until our lips are barely an inch apart. I want to move in, erase that inch and kiss him.

His eyes are vibrantly green today — the color of freshly mowed grass, a beacon of hope on the dreariest of days. But they are weary as if all of this is too much for him too.

I don't trust him to be my hope when I've never gone out seeking for it before. I didn't go looking the night we hooked up, yet I must have felt it because I would have never gone home with him if it wasn't there. Then I picked up on it at his house, and I want to reach out and grab it now.

Badly.

Logan Mitchell can't be trusted with the one thing I want someone to have. My heart, and that right there sweeps hope away with the sudden gust of warm wind.

He is who he is, and I'll never be enough for him.

Tears gather in my eyes. I'm not sure if it's because I can't forgive him for deceiving me, if it's from me being careless and going home with a stranger, or if it's from not breaking down yet and having a good cry.

Logan suddenly entering my life is a cold reminder my past is slithering somewhere out there and threatening to consume my life. And, I don't want him to be that to me. I want him to be as real as he claims. I want to believe every word he says.

It's enough to drive anyone insane.

My heart jumps and swells when he lifts an arm and collects the lone tear that escapes down my cheek. My body wants to react and lean into his hand as he palms my face and rubs a thumb along my jaw. "I don't deserve an apology or an explanation. It's me who owes one to you. The last thing I ever want to do is make you cry. You're scared of a lot of things, and I understand why."

I doubt it. Logan might know Shadow. I know him better. He's ruthless. The spawn of the Devil himself and he will kill me ten times over if and when he finds me.

If he doesn't know already.

"I am sorry for not being honest with you. For walking away without easing your mind. The disgust you have for me makes me hate myself. I need you to forgive me, Ellie. Not sure if I could live with myself if you don't." His voice is soft and sincere. Much different than the man who stood over me at his party.

When Logan's chest heaves as if getting those words out lifts a heaviness that has been holding him back from taking a full breath, I swear I feel the guilt leave his body.

I don't know how long we stay this way. Long enough for me to capture the way he looks at me as if there is nothing else more important in the world than watching me. As if his peace of mind is relying on my forgiveness.

If I forgive him, then what happens next? Is he going to dump me at Shadow's doorstep the first chance he gets? Is he going to think I'll allow him to fuck me and others too? I'll never agree to that, not in this lifetime.

Confusion swarms through me. I have an overwhelming urge to ask him so many questions. I just don't know where to start.

If he wanted to hurt you, he would have done it by now. Norah's words send me reeling while mine fall away due to the sharp edges poking inside my chest. Danger trumps lust and I need to embrace it.

Thunder cracks, becoming a long rolling rumble filling the air with the pending storm. I wait for more, for a surge of lightning to follow, to spark energy that usually expresses itself letting you know to take cover. Instead, the current charge is coming off of Logan and me.

A jagged bolt is striking right through me.

My God.

A surge that shakes me to my core, letting a little more of not understanding what in the hell is happening between us sink under my fevered flesh.

Logan might be a man worth the risk. He might be a man to break my heart, but with every breath he takes, I'm running toward the eye of his storm and head-on into danger. I want to be picked up and taken away with it — a dizzy out of control spiral into the unknown.

"I forgive you. I don't find you disgusting, Logan, not in the slightest." It's true; I don't. He intimidates me, and his way of life is something I won't even dip a toe in. His many secrets I'm sure he's hiding frighten me, however, I have a strong sense there's a lot more to Logan Mitchell than the eye can see.

I think there's good underneath him and he needs a push to expose it. I don't know if I'm the one who can do it. Not when I want a man to be faithful to me.

There's something incredibly sexy about this man, beyond his good looks and rock hard body that draws me in. It's a bad idea being attracted to him this way because everything about Logan has me twisted around.

"Thank you. Go out with me. We can go somewhere private right now and talk. I'll tell you anything you want to know. I'll answer every question, Ellie. I'm taking off to Atlanta for a few days. On business only. I'll cancel if that's what you want, and we can go to your place now if it comforts your mind." A knowing smirk lifts at one side of his mouth.

I don't really know Logan hardly at all. Something tells me the word business was meant to ease my mind. It doesn't, not when it comes to Logan's business. Pleasure is a big part of it, which makes me want to tell him to stay.

Trouble.

I'm heading straight toward it at the speed of a freight train.

Recklessness derived out of passion.

God, please don't let this be a mistake. Don't let me hope and wish and need a man like Logan Mitchell out of loneliness and vulnerability.

I'm more sensible. I have to be.

"Don't cancel your trip, Logan. I won't go out with you until everything is laid out on the table. After that, it's my decision to make. You won't coerce me into going anywhere with you."

The man is persistent; he's deserving of that.

He chuckles. "Pretty sure you'll be the one doing all the driving, sweetheart. You just don't realize it yet."

A sexual innuendo. It goes right between my legs.

Pulsing.

Damn him.

"Well, if I'm driving, let's stay on course. There's something I need to know before you leave. Does Shadow know I'm in New Orleans? Does he know anything about me?" I know I sound like a bitch; I have a right to be scared of everything when it comes to Shadow.

I had a life ahead of me before Shadow took it from me. Ten years wasted, a body afraid to be touched, a scared mind, and more. The impact of him lurking out there will eventually have me committed.

My lips tremble. I'm going to lose it. Tears and a shattering cry is what I need to cleanse myself of the fear setting my safe world off kilter. I balance myself as steady as I can, drawing my inner turmoil tight, pulling those strings and gripping them until I get home where I can break in the confines of my bedroom. Bury my face and not let Norah catch onto the breakdown boiling and bubbling over.

"No. I wouldn't be leaving if he did. You're safe, Ellie. I'm not a good man, but I'm a man of my word."

He eyes me cautiously and caringly as sweat trickles down his temples and neck. The man is soaking in sweat, and his shirt clings to his chest, giving me a peek of how big and muscular it is. It lightens my heart he's sitting out here with me sweating his ass off and not giving two shits about being uncomfortable when he has to be.

Relief hits my system, placing a little calming to the shakes inside. Even so, there's something about the timing of Logan suddenly appearing in my life that doesn't sit well with me. I want to ask more, need to know everything to ease my mind or, set fire to the life I've built and burn it to the ground, but I won't do that here.

"I believe you." This time I do.

Those eyes of his fill with relief. The next words expelling from his mouth add sparks to the air. I swear with the way heat rolls right up my body, they light a match underneath my feet.

"You're everything good, Ellie, and I have never had a slice of it in my life. No matter what you think of me, you can't fault me for wanting to grasp hold of it and hang on."

"Logan, you don't even know me." My heart leaps into my throat, and I stop myself from reaching out to touch the scruff on his face, to grab hold and kiss the man.

"Part of the point of me being here. I'm telling you the truth. I meant it when I said I go after what I want."

I've no doubt he gets everything he wants. It's why *me* that worries me beyond the brink of mental exhaustion.

"When we talk, it will be in private — the same as when I fuck you again. But kissing you, that I'll do anytime, anywhere I please. You were turned on the second you saw me a few minutes ago, the same as I was when I stood across the street and spotted you. I came here to tell you everything about Shadow and found you sitting here. I couldn't take my eyes off of you, Ellie. Deny us all you want. You and I are going to happen. I'm going to remove any doubt, strip the distrust you have for me away and make you see just how good we can be. One chance is all I'm asking for."

My panties flood and my face heats.

It's unexplainable how my senses overload whenever I'm near him. I want Logan the way I had him before and in many other ways. With complete attention on me and no one else.

Wild and uncontrolled.

I want what he's offering more than anything. To make me understand why him out of all men is the one who I allowed to touch me. I need him to help with this undeniable, unexplainable attraction we have.

It's utterly ridiculous when I have this deep feeling getting to know him would crush me.

Even so, his teaching and his reputation have me shaking at the knees. I won't vent my concerns at the moment, not when my life is more valuable than the many women I'm sure he's slept with before and will after me.

I need peace in my mind before we talk about anything else.

"I was turned on because you flare something inside me like nothing else."

Don't go to Atlanta; my head screams back. Jumping ahead of my body and holding a hand up to halt and waggle a finger in my face. I inwardly sigh, Logan does turn me on. I must be crazy to want a little of his bossy, and my body is most definitely on board. It's my brain, my past that's positioned in the forefront that, for the time being, is holding me back from leaping.

"Let me walk you home before it starts pouring, and before this conversation steers in a direction neither of us should be driving into. Not until you know everything. After that, don't expect me to hold back." Logan pushes to his feet, and I take hold of his outstretched hand. He catches his lip between his teeth as his gaze traces over me, passionately and thoroughly.

"Fuck," he murmurs.

Every cell in my body sets aflame — heat and lust and more of that safety as we walk down the sidewalk and stop in front of the side door leading to my apartment.

I'm so out of my element I don't know what to say. I turn around, deciding just to say goodbye when Logan snaps and the next thing I know he's pinning me to the brick wall of my building. He presses in, and when I look up at him, his lids are hooded, jaw set in a firm line.

"I'm sorry for fucking up, never will I be sorry for this or anything that happens between us from here on out. This is me just getting started when it comes to you."

I let out a low moan as he grips the back of my neck, hot mouth claiming mine, prying my lips open and plunging his tongue inside. He licks and fucks me with his tongue. I sink into his kiss, our lips sliding against each other. He directs my mouth, tilting my head and then moving his hands to cup my face.

I am at a complete and utter disadvantage, lost in Logan Mitchell's mouth. Shockingly, yet hungrily so. I whimper, gripping hold of the collar of his shirt as he plunges, seeking, and exploring every inch of my mouth. He kisses me until we're both panting, chests heaving with want as the rain begins to fall, soaking us until we're both drenched. The storm crackling and roaring above.

When he finally pulls away, he leaves his hands where they are, his fingers gently stroking my cheeks. I barely have time to come up for air before he's right back at it again.

When he ends the kiss, he keeps his hold on me, his lips remaining so close, his words catching in my heavy breaths and I inhale them. "I can't stop thinking about you, Ellie. Whatever this is between us, it's the best thing that has ever happened to me. I won't let go of it. Lock yourself inside, sweetheart, and prepare yourself for me to not only prove myself but to prove you are the only woman I need."

I do as he says and the minute I step through my apartment door and find Norah gone, I don't cry.

Because that kiss, it tingled my lips throughout the rest of the night.

CHAPTER 6

Logan

"I hated to leave Ellie wondering. I should have stayed and gotten on my hands and knees and begged her to steal away. I'd have taken her to the one place no one knows about except a few of you. Possibly give her back a little of her childhood while destroying her at the same time."

The second Ellie closed the door and locked herself inside, I almost changed my mind about coming to Atlanta. Hell, it's been hours since I kissed her, several drinks later and I can still taste her on my tongue.

I can't seem to shake the ache in my chest from not coming completely clean about Shadow. Dropping that bomb would have led to questions I wasn't prepared to answer. Not until I talk to the man I came here to see. Worse. When I do, I'm going to turn around and hurt her. I'm beginning to wonder if I'm no different than Shadow in wanting something and knowing I'm going to destroy it.

"I hear you comparing yourself to that rapist. You are nothing like him, do you hear me? Beating yourself up about what you've done isn't helping what you need to do. You can feel guilty for not being honest with Ellie, don't you dare put what Shadow did on you. We've been down that road, not about to go there again."

I swallow around the lump in my throat as I glare across the desk at a man who's like me in many ways. A clusterfuck of emotions pelting me from all sides.

It was right here in this very room where I met Rocco Altieri, the owner of a sex club. He's decked out in his standard black leather, and at one glance most people are shaking in their shoes. The guy is a giant and scary as all hell with his heavy dark beard, long hair and scar across his forehead. But he's all heart and brains with those he cares about and just the man I need to remind me why the thin ice under my feet could give way at any time. Rocco and I have been through some crazy and hellish times together. The only man I've shared a woman with back in our younger days, on several occasions. He's one of the very few people I trust, and someone I don't have to mask my emotions with.

Weak. That's what I feel right now — many variations of it. I'm not ashamed, just not sure how to handle it.

"Ellie isn't safe from me, from the people I've trained, from things I've done. I appreciate you preaching about guilt. We both know that will never go away." I barely squeeze all those words past my lips.

They leave a bad taste in my mouth.

Toxic.

That's what I felt drip into my blood when I heard Ellie mention something about searching for information. The longer I sat with her, the more I knew she wasn't searching me, if she had, she would have gotten up and came at me with what she would have found. All it'll take is typing my name, and a whole slew of shit will come up. Including that goddamn secret.

She was seeking out Shadow. Bet my life on it.

I lied to her again too. I don't have anyone covering up my sins. Sinning is what made me rich. Hell, I had women coming at me from all over the world. Traveled everywhere at their expense just to teach them how to keep a man happy. I've fucked single, engaged, and married women. Not once did I give a shit about who I slept with.

Until Ellie Wynn.

"The fuck are you going on about?"

"This life we chose. You got women you fuck on the regular here. I have them back in New Orleans. Word travels fast, fairly certain they know by now I'm off limits. Some will stop at nothing to destroy Ellie, which means getting word to Shadow. You get what I'm saying now?"

I don't have to remind him of my secret. He knows. That's part of what's troubling me. The worst is some woman or Shadow doing what happened to Rocco.

Thinking they own someone in ways no one should be owned. Women want me for my money. Shadow wants Ellie out of some sick obsession. It's enough to twist my gut.

The scrutiny and sadness in his eyes tells me he understands. A few years ago, Rocco had given up this lifestyle, was ready to walk away from managing even when his woman Sofia trusted him, a woman he'd met in the grocery store of all places. They fell in love. Had it all and then the next thing we knew Sofia was killed right in front of him by a woman from Rocco's past. Bitch wanted Rocco to herself. It's the weirdest thing how I'm sitting in the same boat today. I'll guarantee a few of them are on the ready to strike the first chance they get.

A thousand scenarios cross my mind as I began to sink with dread and the need to get back to Ellie. That memory though, the one where I witnessed something that will haunt me forever, it hits me as if it was yesterday.

Lane and I flew here when Seth called to tell us what went down. For days I watched Rocco fall apart behind closed doors. The minute I thought he was starting to pull out of his funk, was the minute he wanted to end his life. Long story short, I went into the very pit I'm gazing at to check on things. I came back to find Rocco with a loaded gun to his head. The hardest thing I ever had to do was talk my friend down. He ended up giving me the weapon, lowered his head and broke down in my arms. I talked him into moving in with me for six months while Seth moved here and ran the place. Taking over this place brought Seth his own kind of hell. One my troubled mind can't even think about.

Suffering and regret. Misery, so much of it, I can feel it—the grief and guilt Rocco will always hold onto radiating off of him. The emotions winding him up.

Jesus Christ, Ellie is in more danger than anyone should be. It's all around her, and she has no goddamn clue, and like the asshole I am, I sat there and gave her my word.

Pathetic. Yeah, I'm beginning to believe I'm just that.

"Hold up a minute and sign this for me, and I'm all yours." Meaning, he's about to tell me how it's going to be.

I need it. Need it because I'm not even close to stable right now. I'm teetering on the border of insane.

"You could have faxed or emailed this shit." I grab a pen, smirking as I do, knowing full well I needed to get my ass here and take care of business. I scratch my name on the doc for a building in New York we've invested in together and move across the room to stand in front of the window. The scenery is one of the best I've seen. It's what happens around it that has me shaking my head.

This club in Georgia is a hell of a lot different from the one we own because it's off the beaten path, about thirty miles south of Atlanta in the middle of a peach grove owned by Rocco's family and unsuspecting to the thousands of people who come by every year to pick or buy peaches.

Most people drive up the long winding driveway and figure the big white farmhouse is where the owners live. It's partially true, Rocco does live here. What they don't realize is what goes down inside this house once the gates leading up to the place open for a whole other type of clientele. Shit goes down here that the Devil might even question.

Debauchery at its fullest.

Sex and heavy into the glorified BDSM on the inside, murder and chaos on the outside, I call it the Devil's playground. There's some fucked up shit that goes down on this four-hundred and eighty-seven acres. Stuff I'm not even privy to. I'd rather keep it that way. Might have done some things to prove I was trustful to get in with certain people who have my back, but the things they do here make what I've done look like child's play.

It was one of the first clubs I ever walked into where the action was nothing but one big giant orgy. I jumped right into the lion's den way before I was old enough to fuck. My mother telling me the more I practiced, the better I'd get. It was fucked up, but I did it because she would have forced it on Lane if I hadn't. I feasted, and the women ate me up. Greedy pussy like you've never seen. That's when I met Rocco. We became instant friends. Brothers for life and I'd take a bullet for him, same as he'd do me.

I used to love this place about as much as Seth does. After meeting Ellie, the thought of having her anywhere near any of my clubs is enough to make me go blind with fury.

"If we'd have talked on the phone, I wouldn't be the friend you need, would I? Do you want to talk about Ellie or Shadow first?" Rocco hands me a drink and takes a seat in front of the blacked out windows surrounding the main room of the club.

My anger and hatred grow more significant as the thought of Shadow becoming a free man sticks me in one hell of a place. Not like I can stand outside a federal prison and blow his head off the minute he passes through the gate. That isn't how prisoners are released anymore. When the time comes, the rapist could be sitting in the back seat of any car pulling out of there. Following him isn't an option either. He might be bat shit crazy, but he knows I want him dead as much as he does me. Bastard has a plan, someone he wrapped around his dick while inside. Wish like fuck I could have found a way to have him killed while he slept in his cell. The thing was, my greedy twitchy hands wanted to snuff his life myself. It's a mistake I'll live with the rest of my life.

Not sure why the memory of a particular day while hanging with Shadow stirs a cold hollow memory inside of me. It just does.

"I'm going to own that girl, going to make her the queen to my whores. Teach them how to be elegant in whatever circumstance they are in. I want to move up in the world. High-class prostitutes."

"Man, you'll never own her." A girl like Ellie should be worshipped to go along with that owning. Shadow doesn't want that with her. No, he wants to ruin her. Surprised he hasn't crept up on Ellie and messed her up before now.

Shadow's eye twitches, I'd noticed he did that a lot when he talked about Ellie. The guy was getting on my last nerve with his crazy talk about a chick who obviously hated his guts. That's the thing when you become obsessed with someone. You believe what you want to and to hell with everyone else. I'm beginning to wonder if my friend isn't a borderline psychopath.

My mind was in a constant scramble to keep track of his every movement. I didn't trust Shadow as far as I could spit, and every time we drove so he could scratch his itch and see Ellie, I had my trigger finger ready to shoot him in the back if he tried stepping out of his car and going into Ellie's house. Didn't give as many fucks as

I'd let slip with this crazy lunatic if killing a man with his back turned to me was wrong or not. The guy was straight up stalking the girl.

"I will, and I'll kill every motherfucker who stands in my way." He didn't even smile, didn't bat a lash, no emotion whatsoever.

Yeah, straight up psycho.

Flames of outrage lick me from all sides. Setting me ablaze, engulfing me in guilt and fury. No matter what happens between Ellie and me, I will never forgive myself for putting this life before hers. Walking away when I knew he'd take something from her one day.

I pinch the bridge of my nose and breathe.

"Tell me what you found out from your guy on the inside." There's venom in my voice, so much of it, I feel a new surge of emotions burning in my veins — a little more of that corruption and how Shadow can get people to do what he wants. Fucker is a smooth talking son of a bitch in the literal sense.

I take a seat next to Rocco, doing my best to remain calm, inhaling as I wait for him to answer me. I put him on finding out everything he could about Shadow over the years. Several years have gone by, and we don't have shit. Now we need information more than ever to find out what's running through his head.

"Not a damn thing. As always, Shadow's remaining tight-lipped, walking the straight and narrow. My guy is doing life, and he still can't get him to open up. You know as well as me Shadow doesn't trust anyone. Not even that bitch of a sister of his. We know he won't be staying with her. Whitney can't even stand on her own two feet, let alone put his ass up. You made sure of that."

True, I did. That woman is as crafty and as cunning as her brother. She's spreading her legs for shelter, food, and water, that I'm sure.

"You let me take care of Shadow, and you worry about Ellie and everything else you got going on. If I find out anything, you'll be the first to know. You have months, man, seems you should be focusing on taming the bitches before they get out of control."

Motherfucker. Like daggers straight in my gut, his words cut deep.

"Had I known you'd guilt-tripped me, I'd never have come."

"Guilt will ruin a man. If I recall, you saved my ass, Logan. I wouldn't be sitting here watching my friend go all soft over a woman if you wouldn't have talked me down. Not saying what you did with Ellie was wrong or right. Knowing you as I do, if you hadn't run into her, you would have stayed away and made sure she stayed safe for the rest of her life. I'm not going to sit here and say you messed up with her, not after what went down between us a few years ago. You do it right, and having someone care in spite of the things you've done. Seeing beyond the flesh and looking inside, it's the best feeling in the world. You slip, and she'll be gone. That happens, and there's no coming back from the hardness."

I'm soft alright, everywhere except my dick, and it isn't from the show happening below us. Not anymore.

The thought I'd be down there in the middle of it if it weren't for Ellie doesn't even stir my cock. The good I have waiting does. Ellie's enough to make me comfortable as I watch an orgy like none other.

"I didn't realize it was her at first. Kept hearing this faint laugh over the music. The minute I caught her eye, it knocked the air out of me. There's a connection there, Rocco. I want it. I've never been hard up for a woman like I am her. It wasn't part of the job to fuck women. I did it because I was a greedy man. I did it because I could. She knows who I am, but she doesn't know half the shit I've done. From my first kiss with Ellie, it felt like more. I'm going to hurt her and yet, I can't make myself stay away." For a moment I'm afraid I've said something that will prompt Rocco to slip back in time, but as he said, I need his friendship, his advice even if it dredges up memories we'd both soon forget.

"It would be messed up if you went after her and continued fucking others. This is one of the instances where I don't wish I were in your shoes. I can't tell you what to do when it comes to opening up to her. It's eating away at you. It's going to rot you from the inside out and eat your conscience, the more you get to know her. We all have pasts, Logan. It's what we learn from them that matters."

And my past could cost me something I never knew I wanted.

"These women you're talking about, if any of them come near Ellie, you let me know. No hesitation, man, you hear me? Bitches piss me off, give them the dick they go all territorial. If they cared, they'd be doing more than spreading their legs." He laughs sarcastically. "They would dish out of kindness. They would show and not tell. Same as a man would. Nah, brother, I don't have a heart when it comes to women who don't give a fuck about anyone or thing except themselves."

I exhale, doing my best to shutter my past down and think of a way to come clean to Ellie. The woman is someone I'm determined to keep.

"Let's hope it doesn't come to that."

Decisions.

They are going to be like flipping a coin, choosing one side or the other, all the while realizing no matter what side you choose, you're going to lose.

CHAPTER 7

Ellie

"So, tell me, baby girl, this man on your mind, did you sleep with him?"

It's a good thing I finished my water, or I'd have spit it all over the table from Renita's blunt question.

I swallow and turn my head toward the window remembering how Logan basically said we were going to happen so convincingly it scares me. I want it though, at least I think I do. At least my body's reaction to him does, but it's more than that. There has to be, and it's figuring that part out that's as confusing to me as the effect he has on me.

I can't seem to stop daydreaming about what my life could be like and the possibilities of a wonderful one if he were mine. That is if I can learn to trust the man.

"Isn't that one of those for me to know and you do not ask kind of questions? How do you know it's a man?" I shift to face her, forcing a laugh. That's all we've been doing all night is giggling over nonsense. Tonight I needed it. Exhaustion has been weighing me down. I don't think I've slept more than two hours straight since Logan's party. I'm ready to crash.

"Mother's intuition, Ellie."

I tear up around the emotion filling my heart. Renita is the type of person to pick up on just about anything. It's one of the many reasons why I love her so much.

Once I moved in with Renita, she kept Norah and me in fits and giggles. One of the many fond memories of my mother she kept instilled in me. It was Renita's way of reminding that even though it hurt my mother was gone, it was good for my soul to keep her spirit alive inside of me by remembering to laugh. My mother always found a way to laugh and smile every day. Renita, she accomplished that and much more.

She's irreplaceable.

Several times we'd laugh so hard we peed our pants. That made us break out in hysterics until our stomachs hurt. We'd dance and sing in the kitchen, each of us with wooden spoons in our hands belting out lyrics to eighties music, laughing back then was and still is the best medicine for the soul, and it's the most freeing thing in the world there is to me.

I need to do it more often.

Renita keeps her eyes on the receipt she's already signed in front of her, red cat-eye reading glasses nearly falling off the tip of her mousey little nose.

She looks ridiculous and couldn't care less — adding on another reason why I love her.

Her lips quirk, a sure sign my fairy godmother knew the answer before she asked, expressing those curious eyes with a side eye indicating she wants me to spill my confession all over this table.

"You've been distracted these past few days. If this man hurts you, I'll kick his ass. Simple as that. Men say they protect what's theirs, well so do I. You're mine in all the ways that count in here." She places her hand over her big and caring heart. "I'm lucky to have you. You can talk to me about anything, Ellie, I don't need to remind you of that."

If I weren't happy over having her all to myself today, she'd have me bursting in tears.

I draw in a freeing breath, debating on how much to tell her. Too much will have her kicking Logan's ass. Not enough and she'll hound me just like her daughter.

There aren't many people in this world like Renita. A woman who would have fought until the last breath left her lungs to get me out of the system. The woman gave me a family, hope, and love when I thought I had no one. I love her fiercely, and I wish I had it in me to tell her all about Logan. I can't. Not until I have answers.

I want to share the news about Elizabeth with Renita too. Her death would have us laughing like two hyenas.

"I'm the lucky one, Renita. His name is Logan. We've just started seeing each other. He, um, owns the sex club where Eric works. It's way past your bedtime, isn't it?" I speak with a tease, lean in, whispering my next words, feeling a flush creep at my cheeks and doing my best not to spill the truth all over our table. "I did sleep with him. I'm not ashamed either. Do you think this is the place to talk about it?" I sigh, think back to the day when all I wanted to do was give up on finding a man who would make me feel something besides disdain for everyone I dated. What happened to me wasn't their fault, and yet every time they touched me, I went home and showered.

I scrubbed until I was excruciatingly red and raw. There were times I split my skin open, and still, I kept on cleansing until blood pooled around my feet.

Funny how when I showered after leaving Logan's, the

last thing on my mind was erasing his scent. I still haven't washed the dress I wore.

"Look at you trying to crack a joke about my age. And there's nothing to feel ashamed about, Ellie. What you do is your business, no one else. We don't have to talk about it at all if you don't want to. I wanted to make sure you were okay, but…" She shoves a copy of the receipt and her glasses in her purse and lifts those caring eyes to mine. "That's quite a leap for you. The man is a—"

I place my hand over her mouth. "I know what he is, Renita. Please don't say it out loud."

Worry shows in the wrinkles around her eyes as they close briefly, only to re-open wide.

I drop my hand at the same time she brings one of hers to cup my cheek. "Okay. I'm not judging the man or you, I'm concerned. You won't stop me from feeling that way, Ellie. I won't lock it down."

"I don't expect you to."

I trust my instinct to spill; I don't trust the man I'm spilling about. It takes the better part of a half hour for me to explain how I met Logan, and what went down after. The only thing I leave out is his association with Shadow. That's too much for her right now.

"Logan, he's, I don't know what he is. He frightens me, but there's something about him that makes me want to learn more. It could be a mistake, Renita. I won't know unless I give him a chance." That's the truth.

"Okay, I'm going to ask a couple of questions and then I'm staying out of your personal life. Safety, please tell me you used it?" Renita's voice is laced with her motherly worry.

"Of course we did." There isn't much of us yet. If things were to get to the point where no protection is brought up, I wouldn't hesitate to ask Logan to show me proof he's safe.

Although, I don't think the man is the type to go around screwing people if he wasn't.

"I figured you did." She gently strokes my cheek. "Do you want Logan or need Logan? There's a difference, Ellie. I don't have to remind you how dissimilar they are."

"I know." I swallow, remembering how she explained just how unlike the two are.

Need is something obtained. A means of survival. Want is something that people wish to have, that they may, or may not, be able to obtain. But like any depravity, we are all of a mind to fall face first into a confined hole full of want than to rise in the chasing of our needs. Put the two together, and the sum is desire.

A yearning that doesn't go away.

"I hope you do, because the first fall is the hardest. Some last forever, others don't, and no matter how old you are, Ellie, I don't want to see you hurt."

I grab hold of the fiery strength and determination Renita gave me to place my feet on the floor every morning and walk. To not let life's unexpected twists knock me down.

But there's also this little thing in my chest called my heart. Telling me Logan would never be faithful to me.

"I don't want to be hurt either, but I'm tired of being lonely. Tired of letting what happened rule my life."

I've been lonely for so long, searching for something when it became severe. I gave up searching long before I met Logan and that's when it happened. The man filling me with hope, branding me with his sin.

I want to be touched, soothed, and talked to. I deserve to find out everything there is to know about someone like I'd hope that someone would want to do with me. I also need a man to keep that fire he lit burning, and Logan did that for me. I might have been out of sorts when we talked, but I felt the spark. Those sinful eyes of his wavering between hunger and regret. The flames of need in the way he reached out and wiped my tear away and the misery in the pinch of his face when we said goodbye.

Now that I've had time to think, I believe Logan would seek deep within me as well as fire me up with one of his numbing kisses, a look from across the table, or an evening filled with sexual innuendos that lead to mind-blowing raw satisfying sex.

It's an opposing contradictory feeling to what I felt when I first found out who he was.

"You deserve to experience what it feels like to be treasured and adored. Worshipped and sated. I don't know this man, but I know you, and you wouldn't have given yourself to him if you didn't feel a connection."

"I felt it."

God did I ever. I can feel it now and he's not even near.

Last night, I told Norah everything and when I climbed into bed, I tossed fitfully. Finally I got up and decided to focus on Logan during my morning swim. I allowed my mind to think the whole situation through, acknowledging these feelings he's stirred inside me and how one passionate night could lead to something great.

Logan is a sexual man. He's not afraid to say what he wants. I have no clue what I want; I only know what I need.

I shoved his past aside. It might be the stupidest move I'll make. His past doesn't mean a thing to me. It doesn't define who he is. It's whether he'll give it up that matters, and I'm sorry to say. I won't go out with him, won't let him touch or kiss me ever again if I'm not fully convinced he will.

So, this morning I called him to find out when he'd be returning from Atlanta, and when it went to voicemail, I left a message, as of yet he hasn't called back.

The chemistry we shared could be all there is. A heartbreak ready to happen before it even starts. Still, I can't take my mind off Logan no matter how much I try, and I don't want to stop thinking about him.

I should be scared to death and stay as far away from Logan Mitchell as I can. I'm not. I'm going with my gut, which tells me this man might have secrets, some I might learn quickly, others may come in time, but I honestly don't believe he's in my life to hurt me. At least, I hope not. And hope, along with staying true to who I am is what will guide me.

Most importantly to me and my sanity, I'll never be free from that heinous night, never stop hearing Shadow's voice or the feeling of my body ripping in two if I don't give in to my desire, if I do, then he and Whitney win in their wicked way of destroying me.

With those thoughts lingering, my heart thuds wildly just thinking about seeing Logan again.

Renita's gaze warms me as we both stand to leave our early dinner date, her lips spreading into a smile.

"You're a grown woman, one I've loved as if you were mine since you were born. Your mother would be proud of you, Ellie. I'm proud of you. I want to tell you something my mother told me when I started dating. She said, when you fall, you'll know because that man, the one you're supposed to be with for life, he'll fight for you when things are bad. He'll hold your hand when life feels like it's too much to handle, and he'll steal your breath, catch your soul, love you, and never tell you a lie. That's what my Jonathon did for me. Our love was short-lived when he died. I've yet to find another. If Logan isn't that man, then the right one is out there somewhere."

A grin plays around my face, and heartwarming tears form in my eyes. I breathe in deep and remember my mother's smile and the way she jumped up and down like a cheerleader, clapping her hands and doing a little dance when I finally mastered diving into the pool during swim lessons. For some reason, hitting water head first scared me. But I wasn't going to give up, swimming was what my dad called family time in the hot summer evenings, and I wanted to learn so that I could race my parents across the length of the pool, and learn I did, and to this day I swim at the local YMCA as much as I can.

Just as quickly, my happy memory vanishes, replaced by my mother's empty eyes when she'd look at me having no clue who I was.

"You might be jumping the gun a bit, Renita. I've only seen Logan three times. I'm far from falling. However, those are wise words from a wise woman."

Renita's husband was killed in a car accident when Norah and I were four. I barely remember him. I remember my mother and me going over to Renita's house where she helped with whatever was needed while Renita cried and cried, and I sat with Norah wanting to play and couldn't quite understand why she was sad. We went back every day for a month, and every day I put new clothes on Norah's dolls and held her hand while my friend's silent tears dripped down her face.

"I'm not jumping the gun; I'm tooting my horn. I raised some smart girls, and I'm taking my old ass home with pride. You get on back to your place. I'll see you Monday morning. I love you."

Right. Tomorrow is Sunday, my day to sleep in, and God do I need it. I've been on an emotional rollercoaster, and I want off.

"And Ellie, listen to your heart. It might get hurt, it might be wrong, but when you open it to the right person, he'll do everything in his power to keep it beating. I promise he will. Don't be afraid to let go and give your body what it craves either. Don't shame yourself for giving in and enjoying the perks of a man; it'll only beat you down if you let it."

I stare at her backside with my mouth gaping open as we walk through the small Italian restaurant, confidence and embarrassment a giant bubble ready to burst in my chest.

Building and building.

"If I do, I won't be sharing a thing with you or Norah. I love you so much, Renita. Thanks for dinner."

Renita turns and flashes me a devious smile as if she wants to spill things about her sex life; my ears will never bleed free.

"Don't say a word."

"Fine. Just know I might not have found someone else to give my heart to; it doesn't mean I still can't tempt and tease and do some taking and shaking of my own."

"Stop." I burst out laughing as she walks away. I wait for her to get in her car before hitting the key fob on my Jeep, crossing the street and climbing in.

Five minutes later, I'm still giggling as I pull into the parking lot next to the store, by the time I climb out, I'm exhausted. I want to take a bath, slip under the covers and rest my mind.

My confidence slips and panic in the form of a cold sweat blankets me like a sheet of ice when I notice a dark SUV slow to a crawling speed until it stops and whips into the parking lot. The black tinted windows put me on high alert. My hands start shaking, my legs wobble. My heart hammers against my breastbone, a painful strike that shortens my breath. Sweat dampens my palms and fear spreads throughout every part of my body as I rush toward the door.

I fumble with my keys trying to get them in the lock, and just as I fling open the door, I'm grabbed from behind and shoved inside. I jump and scream, nerves tattering at the ends when it slams shut.

Terror.

It blares in my ears.

Unceasing and unrelenting as it splinters my thoughts and grips hold of my senses.

The hairs on the back of my neck rise when a man with a ski mask over his head snarls and licks his lips through the small hole around his mouth.

I blink, steadying my glare to make sure those eyes aren't Shadow's.

They aren't, still, dread beats like a drum in my bloodstream, the impact of what could happen to me again jars me to my bones.

Everything I learned in the self-defense classes Renita, Norah, and I had taken evaporates from my mind. The only thing I recall is how fearful I was when Shadow hurt me, how I crawled on my hands and knees the rest of the way home. The tears wouldn't stop falling. They blurred my swollen eyes over what I lost. My legs, knees, and palms were scraped and covered in blood. My mind wondering how anyone could be cruel enough to destroy a person's life. I vaguely remember Renita falling to the ground and holding me when I finally reached the end of our driveway and screamed for help.

Filthy. I felt it stab holes into my bones, and it's drilling into them now.

Old memories crash into my skull, the examination, the police questions, bright white lights and the way I just wanted to die.

A cry rips from my mouth when the man reaches for me. Curling a hand around my wrist, his fingers pressing painfully into my flesh.

Fear floods my veins, pushing through as if it wants to escape this stairwell. I wish it would and take me with it.

I scream when he grabs hold of my throat in a brutal grip

as he shoves me against the wall, presses his body against mine, and throwing my mind into the nightmare of my past.

"Get off me." I chance a glance into his eyes and see punishing intent, wickedness like none other. This man will kill me with one snap of my neck and not think twice.

I whimper, my fright reaching in and strangling my strength.

A fist connects with my cheek and knocks me to my knees — the air escaping from my lungs.

Get up, Ellie. You are stronger than this. You kill him if that's what it takes.

"You bastard." My voice wobbles around my gasping. All I can see, all I can feel when my fear courses through me is the monster who took my innocence away — the evil in his voice, the laughter, his grunts, and groans. The satisfaction I felt rolling off of Shadow as he tore through me.

I flinch, my face erupting into flames when he bitch slaps me. I try shutting my mind down from the memories of what happened to me before. I try remembering every trick I was taught to protect myself, but when he kneels in front of me, my recollections of being attacked have me gasping for air.

I can't breathe.

"You're a hot little piece of ass; maybe I should take a piece of it."

No! I won't let that happen again. I will not allow a man to take from me ever again. I'm in charge of who I give myself to. I will fight this crazy son of a bitch with all I have.

I swallow the bile in my throat and meet his eyes. "Touch me, and I'll shoot you." I reach for the gun in my bag only to have him jerk it out of my hand and fling it to the floor.

"Not if I kill you first." His eyes narrow and a hand slides up my thigh.

My chest tightens, and freezing shots of terror that

mirror my breathlessness take over, a cold, nauseous sensation pricks at my ribs.

I can handle this man hitting me, but unwanted hands, I cannot.

Fury, it burns right through me.

Lifting my head and my hands, I cuff the man in his face, I scratch at his eyes, pushing them as far into his warped brain as I can. Terrifying sounds tear from my throat, fingernails scraping at his cheeks. He jerks on my hair, and I suck in a lungful of air at the excruciating pain in my scalp.

I'll survive or die trying. No matter what this psycho does to me, no matter the fact I'm in an enclosed area where no one can hear me, I'll never give up. Not until the last breath leaves my lungs.

He grips both of my hands in one of his, the other grabbing hold of my jaw.

"Fucking little cunt. When was the last time you were properly fucked?"

My body freezes and my mind races.

I don't say a word, hoping he'll leave. He doesn't, but what he said is running through my head like a nightmare. Terror curls through my veins in freezing gushes at the reality that the man intends to tear into me.

My stomach flips on itself as hairs on the back of my neck stand on end. His hand comes up and the next thing I know, I'm hit in the temple and flying sideways, landing on the stairs leading to my apartment with a loud crack and a throbbing jaw.

Bitterness drains, it stiffens my spine and knows no bounds. I've no idea where it comes from, but I welcome it like a flame. I kick at the attacker, knocking him back on his ass.

"I'll do you from both ends for that. One warning you little bitch. Stay away from Logan Mitchell."

My body freezes and my mind races.

Did one of those women from Logan's party send this man to scare me away? Well fuck them, I'll do as I damn well please. I now possess a hatred that makes me want to hurt whoever sent this asshole to threaten me.

Tears blur his yellowing smile as he pushes up and towers over me.

A sob rips from my chest.

My head spins, and vision fades. I swear I feel the temperature rise like someone opened the door. Lifting my head, my gaze darts toward the man, and I don't know whether the dark figure standing in the doorway is my savior or a partner to this evil man.

I hear the cock of a gun. The sound of cursing and then everything goes black.

CHAPTER 8

Logan

Wrath unfolds and covers my insides, attempting to convince me to kill without getting the information I need, the sweet taste of doing just that climbing up my throat. Not that I'll get what I want. Most people who know they're about to die, tend to clamp up or spew lies to try and save their ass. This cocksucker has been doing a bit of both.

Teasing and twisting my guilt a little further.

My own bottle of toxic.

It's now trying to poke through Ellie.

"I'm guessing your momma didn't teach you not to put your hands on a woman without permission."

"Fuck you," the guy snarls.

He already did by putting his dirty hands on Ellie.

"Man, you have nowhere to go but hell from here. You may as well tell me what I want to know or die a painful death from being burnt alive."

This asshole's smug grin has me clenching my fists while all the ways he could've violated Ellie loop around my brain, leaving me a violent pissed off man.

My anger increases, howling and doing its best to swallow me whole. I knew this would happen, didn't think someone would stoop this low as to have Ellie attacked. I should have shut my feelings down, should do it and leave her be before they take this violence further.

It won't do me any good, obviously whoever set this atrocious plan in motion set out to do more than scare her away. Makes me want to shower her with protection all the more. She'll have it too.

Never have I wanted to yank out someone's jugular and crush it in my hands the way I want to destroy whoever hired this fucker.

Punishment. An old-fashioned settling of scores by death.

"Let's try this again. Did you happen to be in the neighborhood or did someone hire you?" I grind out for the third time, lift my booted foot and nail this stupid moron in the balls — chuckling as he tries wrapping his arms around his stomach but fails when I lodge my arm underneath his throat, pressing on his windpipe.

He sucks in a gasp of air, his body tightening with all the commotion I imagine is creating some frightened ruckus inside his head. Little prick knows he's going to die.

"That has to burn like a bitch. You're lucky I don't cut it off. Limp-dick motherfucker."

"Shit; damn it." He pants, coughing and sputtering — eyes bulging out of his ugly mug.

"I'm just getting started, buddy."

"What the hell does that mean? Are you going to kill me?" Sweat beads across his forehead, his face turning white as snow, stark against his bloodstained Cajun speaking lips.

"What do you think it means? You messed with something that's mine."

Even if Ellie weren't on my radar, I'd hope someone

would find a way to nail his balls to the wall. Can't stomach a man putting his hands on a woman with intent to cause her harm.

God, this is going to set rage a filthy shade of red in Rocco like nothing else. If I see red, he's going to bleed it until whoever did this dies.

Releasing my hold on his throat, I begin punching his face, nearly pummeling it in. My hands burn with every punch I throw as he tries fighting me off. The blood from his face splatters onto my clothes. My knuckles split and sting, and still, I don't stop, not until I've released enough pent-up anger searing through me out on him.

Blood drips like the current of the Mississippi from this fucker's broken nose and his split lip and if he doesn't tell me the truth next time I ask, I'll make him mentally suffer until he shits his goddamn pants.

I flip open his wallet, lift it toward the dashboard to catch his name on his ID. Marty Sutter. Dumb name for a foolish fuck who got caught.

"I'm telling you, I met a woman with long blonde hair at Slackers on 8th and Weston. We got to talking and she asked me to rough the woman up a bit, so I did."

A blonde? If he's telling the truth that rules out most of the women I know because I hate fucking blondes. Haven't touched one in years. The only blonde I care about is my niece who barely comes up to my knees, and if anyone laid a hand on her the way this punk did Ellie, he'd be living his last minutes the same way as this guy.

He isn't a professional killer. If he were, he wouldn't have gotten caught. I lived with one for several years, know how the mind of an assassin works. This one's an amateur. He's a piece of trash. A desperate one that whoever convinced him to do this picked him up at a seedy bar or off the streets.

I've seen enough evil in my life to know if Seth wouldn't have gotten there in time, Ellie would have gotten hurt in ways she might never have recovered from.

My stomach roils in outrage of what could have happened.

"Bullshit." I plow my fist into his jaw, his head jerking sideways before slamming back into the headrest. "You give me a name, or you're going in the river, and I'll let the leeches and snakes kill you instead of me. Pussies like you going around physically hurting women don't deserve to live."

I chuck a thumb behind me to where Seth is standing at the back of the car ready to push the guy's vehicle over an old unused railroad track into the river. Won't be a few minutes before the deep muddy, toxic water sucks it under.

Hot burning anger seethes and seeks to harm. I've killed and dumped a few bodies in The Mississippi before, and I'll do it again and again if need be. I wasn't born to be a natural killer; some things just have to be done to survive.

"The only name she gave me was yours. Sure hope my threat for your beautiful little piece of ass to stay away digs deep."

I snarl as my fury roils with enough anger I could explode, and my head goes to battle with my heart. If Ellie runs from me because of this, there's no telling what I'll do. Shut every damn club down so this crazy shit doesn't happen to anyone else who might want out.

Fucking Christ.

"Looks to me like the woman you attacked didn't take all that kindly to your threat." I can't help the chuckle that escapes my mouth. Ellie dug the hell out of his face.

Good for her.

I had no sooner boarded our small jet, a man on a mission to get back to Ellie after hearing her voicemail asking when

I'd be getting back to town when Seth called to tell me someone attacked her. I tried calming him down and ended up calling Lane because guilt was dripping from every word Seth spoke.

He had followed Ellie home and started to drive by when he saw a vehicle half-assed parked by her door. It took him a minute to turn around and get to her. A minute is a long damn time when you have nowhere to run. I can't even begin to imagine how frightened she was.

Her family's hodge-podge store is an everyday mother's dream. One that says I love my family more than anything except I need a break and I know the perfect spot to go. Crime doesn't happen in her small little neck of New Orleans. The idea of her living there alone even when it's busy has driven me mad. The thing is, it seems like it's Ellie, a simple life filled with commotion and now someone has tainted it.

My mind had tumbled into a violent rage by the time I made the rest of the short flight from Atlanta.

For the first time in my life, I'd begun to decompress my mind and not let some of the things I've done get to me. I was going to tell her everything and then get on my hands and knees and beg for forgiveness. Rage blistered my muscles when I thought of someone else so much as touching her. I couldn't stop thinking about her. Ellie is my obsession and it's not in a sick and twisted way like some would think. She's like sweet venom seeping into my brain and taking over, and I need to get to her. First, I need to kill this asshole who dared to touch her.

A moving, emotional image of Ellie's face caught up in worry and fear, and the pounding of her heart, loop around my spine, sending needle-like pricks across my back. Her desperate screams Seth said he'd heard switch into horrifying cries of terror and blast so damn loud in my ears that I need her in my arms to quiet the racket.

It's all kinds of fucked when I don't understand how I can feel this way about her in such a short amount of time. Maybe it's because through the years I worried about her. Fuck all if I know. What I sure as hell am sure of is I'm not letting Ellie slip through my fingers.

"I've dealt with men like you — the ones with no one around to give a fuck whether you die. There won't be a soul out there who will miss you. Consider yourself lucky I don't snap your goddamn fingers off and shove them up your ass. How much were you paid?"

It doesn't matter if he received a million; he isn't going to live to spend it.

Money rules out Whitney because the bitch doesn't have any. It has to be some jealous bitch from the club.

I angle in farther, grab the guy by the collar and pull him into me. Sweat drips down his face, his temples pulsing at the side of his neck. His small brown eyes twitch as he glances briefly from me to Seth and back again.

"Yeah, asshole, you are so deep in the woods, so far out of the city, even the smoky colored moon doesn't give off much light. There's nothing out here but wild animals and carnivores. Crocodiles and gators, no bright light to lessen the darkness on your soul."

"Five hundred and her mouth wrapped around my dick." He grins, spits a wad of blood onto the ground and swallows. "You want the truth; I'll lay it out for you. Killing me won't be the end of this. Think about it, man, any woman seeking out and hiring someone to rough someone up isn't going to stop there. Bitches are catty and jealous. Whatever you did to piss the woman off, you must have done it well."

Might be true, it doesn't stop the repulsion, the self-hatred seeping through my skin.

They grow. Sinking into my body with a stinging bite of reality and flinging me into the dark depths of my past.

Whoever hired him could be anyone. I used to fuck more women in a month than there are days. Makes me sick this was done by a woman scorned by me. If and I mean, if, he's telling the truth about it being a woman.

I'll do whatever it takes to make sure what happened to Sofia doesn't happen to Ellie. Shit's sake, how can someone become twisted and obsessed this way? Why not open up and tell me how they feel instead of doing wrong?

Goes to show how deranged some people can be over sex, money, and power.

My blood runs cold. I need this man taken care of, so I clean the blood off my hands and check on Ellie.

"I've met men like you too, asshole. You think you are so much better than the rest of us. Tossing money around, women dropping like flies at your feet. I know who you are. The rich bastard, fucking women that pay thousands for. You are nothing but a male whore. Ask me, that woman is too damn good for you."

"I didn't ask."

I'll figure it out and whoever hired him will soon know not even their pitiful attempt won't keep me away from her. The second I sunk inside that tight little body, Ellie became mine.

"That's right, motherfucker; I'm a man. An invisible one who is saving this city from someone like you. A limp dick who gets off by roughing up a woman."

Cocking the gun I found on him, I place it against his temple and start the car. The man turns and takes a swing at me, clocking me in the jaw and causing me to stumble.

Fuck that stings.

"I'll find out who hired you. That, you can count on." I pull the trigger nailing him between his eyes, slam the door, pull off my leather gloves and help Seth push the car into the water.

Right there I vow whoever hired him will die an even harsher death.

CHAPTER 9

Ellie

Rolling over, I bury myself a little more under the covers and take a few calming breaths in hopes the pain throbbing around my skull would listen as I will it to go away. Lifting a hand, I press my palm against my face. It's slightly swollen and warm, but I'm in one piece, and thankfully someone stopped the man from taking a part of me I don't think I'd be able to come back from like I did before.

Blinking against the sunlight, I open my eyes and glance at the clock to check how long I've been out and wonder how the hell I got out of my clothes, into my sleep shirt and my bed. With an abundance of gratitude, I let out a contented sigh to whoever the man was that showed up and saved me.

If only someone like him would have been around to save me before.

The sky is a pale blue, wisps of white clouds unmoving and notched with the promise of life in a world of darkness, a sense of warmth as I shift my gaze to the terrace window.

They do nothing to calm the cold, brutal lashing of my heart, especially when I take another deep breath and smell *him*.

Every muscle in my body seizes up, and it's not from struggling to get rid of my headache. It's because Logan is in bed with me. I can feel the heat radiating off of his arms as they curl around my stomach. I can feel his eyes on the back of my head, his restraint not to grind the thick bulge between his legs that's pressed against my ass.

He sets me on fire, giving me an instant fever that shoots to a risky level. I hate the way my body is reacting when inside I should be angry; it's a thrill that ticks me off and makes me consider calling my old therapist to have my head examined.

My mind is screaming asking why is this happening to me. While my heart is enjoying the safety of his arms. It's fleeing away from me when everything else is commanding me to run. My nerves are drawn tight; I'm edgy and angry that I like Logan when a part of me screams I shouldn't. I'm frightened I'll have that cry. I hold my breath until I feel dizzy, then let it out and grab onto the strength I have, all the while wondering how much more can I take before I break?

I can picture Logan now. Apprehension is filling his mind as he tries to capture my thoughts. I wish he could because then I could lie here in the safety of his arms and forget that someone wanted to hurt me.

A rile of aggravation swells inside of me as his breathing hitches, and silence lingers. I want to tell him to start talking or get the hell away from me, but the part of me drawn so profoundly to him finds comfort in him being here.

"What happened to you is my fault. I'm sorry. It seems those two words keep coming out when it comes to you. My brother Seth was keeping an eye on you while I was out of town. It has nothing to do with Shadow, it has to do with me. Seth overheard the threat, knocked out the guy who attacked you and found Norah's number in your bag. He called her, then called me. She checked you over and put you to bed. You have a slight bruise on the side of your face and a small cut below your eye. I promise you I'll find whoever is responsible and it won't happen again. No man's hands but mine will ever touch you again, Ellie."

I hear the fear in his voice, not at all like the controlling man he is.

A smile tugs on my lips. Equally fragile as it is thankful. For the reason that there's sorrow in the way Logan says his brother's name. A story is there. One of heartache and sadness. I can sense Logan carries the heaviness of it on his shoulders as clear as the sky is blue.

"Tell him thank you."

I wait in silence. I might be grateful, but he's the one who owes me words.

"I need you to hear me; feel me for just a minute, Ellie."

His words nearly become my breaking point because there, in his plea, is a man on the edge of his.

Logan nips the nape of my neck, his hot breath fogging my level of logic. I moan just as he scrapes his teeth across the sensitive flesh. "I'm sorry. A thousand apologies will never be enough."

Tears slide down my temples; I swipe them away. I should bolt out of this bed and make him leave. I'm sure he either hurt or killed the man who attacked me. I'm sure Logan is far more dangerous than I thought and yet here I stay, pushing my ass into his erection and emitting a growl from his mouth and several swipes of his tongue across my neck.

I don't think this is what Renita meant by giving in to my body's needs, but God does it ever feel good.

"Are you alright?"

I nod, a lump stuck in my throat.

"You're mine, Ellie. Don't try pushing me away, don't try

escaping, I won't allow it. You want me as bad as I do you. You smell so good, so edible that all I can think of is how good you're going to taste. How that mouth of yours that wants to tell me to go is going to sound when I sink my teeth into your smooth flesh."

Goosebumps race along my skin as I slowly shift to face him. None of what happened to me seems real anymore. At least not with him here. I might not know this man, but the one thing I'm positive about is Logan is a man who protects.

And at this moment as I stare into his tired eyes, I know he's right. I want to be his, this man who keeps showing up — the only one who has ever consumed my mind.

Regardless of any of that, he's going to respect me at the moment, or he'll be high tailing his ass right out of here.

He sucks in air, and I whimper when my hands touch his bare chest. My fingers are trembling as I run my palms up and down his smooth skin.

Colorful tattoos I didn't have the opportunity to study the night we met cover parts of his chest and arms.

"You're shaking. Are you frightened of me?"

I should pull away, but I find myself moving closer to him, unable to break the lock of our stares. Logan has the most beautiful shade of eyes I've seen. A forest I wouldn't mind being lost in.

"I'm not afraid of you; I'm afraid of what you'll do to my heart. I'm afraid of Shadow finding me. I'm afraid you want me to kneel at your feet, Logan. I'm afraid you want control of me, and I don't want someone to control me. I want an equal. I've always told myself a man wouldn't own me unless I want to be, but somehow you make me want to be. We're alone now; there's no excuse for you not to tell me everything."

A heaviness settles over him. Watchful eyes emotionless,

mouth set firm, jaw stiff as if he were choking down what he wants to say.

Maybe I should be scared.

"I want to know who sent someone to attack me; I won't give in to anyone trying to scare me. I've lived in fear most of my life; I won't live there again. I want to know why you want me so badly. I won't fall for you and have you talk me into sleeping with others. I won't share you either. I suggest you start talking or you can go. Someone sent me a warning, and you owe me the truth as to why." I decide to throw all my concerns at him at once to study his expression and gather it all in my mind.

His chest heaves and his features crack wide open to expose the man hidden underneath — a man who isn't used to someone telling him what to do. I see a vulnerable side to Logan too, and it's me. The weighty sounds of his breathing and the sight of his pulse fluttering desperately in his throat remind me to breathe.

I battle to steady my breathing while I try to ignore the magnetism of the man before me, his struggle to remain under control, the slight twitch at the corners of his mouth, and his expression is a picture of uncertainty.

It should be. This crazy chemistry is not enough to keep me bound to him.

A sudden blaze of regret flashes in his eyes as he leans in until our lips are almost touching. If I weren't breathing hard and fast, I'd swear he'd steal the breath from my lungs.

What on God's green earth is wrong with me? Because the only thing I want at this moment is to climb inside of him and cling to safety.

"Shadow doesn't belong in this bed with you and me. Understand this; he will never be talked of when I have you in bed again. First, you need to be set straight when it comes to my intentions with you. Never fear me."

His fingers trail through my hair, and he watches his movement as if he can't believe I'd even speak to him after this.

Quite honestly, I can't either.

"Listen close because I won't repeat myself when it comes to this subject again. What I've done isn't as wrong as it is illegal, it's a lifestyle I've enjoyed. It's exhilarating, and there's so much more to what happens inside Behind Closed Doors than what most people know, but only if a person wants it. I won't ask for forgiveness when the things I've done were before I met you. I will ask you to forgive me for bringing you into a complicated lifestyle; you should have known before I brought you to my bed. That I won't apologize for anymore."

I say nothing as I watch the rise and fall of his chest. I want this man, need him even though I'm afraid he'll hurt me.

I'm crumbling.

I feel another wall rattle and shake. More pieces are falling and crashing to the ground.

"There are plenty of women who come in to play. Unicorns are what the lifestyle calls them. They swing both ways. Plenty of them lie about not having a significant other and…"

An uproar of bile spools in my gut while Logan takes a deep breath.

"I've made unintentional enemies out of boyfriends and husbands. There's also the women who want me for themselves. I'd like to believe I'm untouchable. I guess the truth is, I'm not. Our club should be fun and adventurous, an exploration into sex. No one should ever be hurt."

I drop my eyes, as if not looking at him will shield me from his words. I stare at the massive chest my palms rest on; it's warm; it feels comforting. So many women have touched this body before me. I don't like it. I also don't like how Logan is a man who doesn't care about vows that I hope someday become the world to me. It unnerves me. I hate it.

Hate I'm even considering taking a chance on a man who cheats.

"I've done a lot of thinking since the night I spent with you. A lot of wondering over the years about you. Knowing where you were and wondering why I had this need to protect you. I wasn't man enough to come forward. I own up to it now. You are brave and beautiful and God, I don't understand any of this. I have demons and ghosts and blood on my hands. You are pure and wholesome and caring. I would never cheat on you, Ellie. I know you don't believe me. I understand why you wouldn't. I haven't been with anyone since you, and if you'd let me in, I'd prove I don't want anyone else. I don't want to share you; I want you to myself. You make me want to change. Make me want more; I want to get to know you so bad. I can't even explain it."

We get hooked in each other's eyes—trapped in want and need. A net waiting to be dragged in and discover what's caught, and it's taking everything in me not to lean up until our lips join. The moment smolders with a chance. Simmers with something that's beyond my control.

It's maddening to me.

"I don't want to understand that kind of life. I don't want to know the rules. I want nothing to do with it. I would never judge or hate or put anyone down for living how they chose, but vows and commitment, they mean faithful to me. I won't be cheated on, in any way, Logan, and I won't turn my back on whatever is happening between us because some jealous bitch threatens me. I will walk if you ever lie to me and no amount of heavy dominating persuasion from you will change my mind."

I don't want to question whether he's honest or not. If I

do, we won't move forward.

God, my mind is so at odds.

Conflict and confusion and scared out of my ever-loving mind.

Everything he said hits me square in the chest.

"I don't deserve a chance."

Maybe not. I'm giving him one anyway. He better not waste it.

I raise my chin and straighten myself out. "Everyone has a past, Logan. You weren't the only one there the night we met. I was as willing as you. Just, please don't make me regret this. Don't make me a fool because I'm giving you the benefit of the doubt. You do, and that will be the day you will underestimate me." I sound territorial. I don't care. I might succumb to other things when it comes to this man. Cheating or using me will not be one of them.

Logan continues to study me, taking his thumb, drawing it lightly under my eye, down my cheek, and across my bottom lip.

His Adam's apple bobs. I want to lick right up his chest and attach my lips to that ball in his throat. My eyes outline the length of his neck, noticing his pulse hammering away, the veined cords straining as I lie here hoping what he said is the truth.

God Almighty. Someone pinch me and tell me I'm utterly crazy for believing him.

"I'd be the fool if I did."

My pulse pounds in my ears, my mind starts a war with itself — every piece of me is battling against the part of me wanting to believe.

My heart.

"Not one of the women I've been with has held my interest the way you do. The only place I would ever ask for the control is in private. Do I want you to kneel? Yes, I do, but only for me. I want to push you until you beg. I'll fuck you until you come so hard you'll hurt, but I'd never ask you to do something you don't want to do. And, I'd never try to change you. I like you the way you are. I don't want you worrying about me being clean either. I am. It's a requirement every member has to prove."

Those words alone have my body in an overwhelming bundle of need.

"I want proof."

Logan's lips twitch, breaking into a devilish smile. "You'll have it."

I feel his command rolling over me. He's potent, and I refuse to let him see how much that terrifies and excites—me.

"This connection between us, Ellie, it's unexplainable. It's magnetic. It's - fuck, I don't know what it is, but I refuse to let you go. The way your body responded to me the night we met. The way it's responding to me now, and how it feels when I'm inside you. I want that again and more. You blew my fucking mind, Ellie Wynn."

Logan grabs my hand, bringing it to his lips and kisses across my knuckles in the same gentle way he did before. The man has a habit of that, and I like it so, so much. "I'll never hurt you, never lay a hand on you without your permission. I promise you that, Ellie. I'll never push you further than your mind or body can handle. I will push you to the edge; I'll leave you dangling until your begging to fall over. I will give you more pleasure than you've ever dreamed possible. You need to trust me, Ellie." The confidence in his voice. The deep tenor of it is seduction on its own.

I gulp down a tug of anxiety when I notice his raw and scraped knuckles, pleading with my mind to allow me to grasp onto the promise Logan will never hurt me.

Promises are empty; they are broken every day. Trust is

something I don't know if I can give completely when my rational thoughts are all over the place. I'm so far out of my league with this man, it's terrifying.

"I don't want to be wanted, Logan. I want to be needed. I want to trust you. I do. You have to earn it the same way as I have to earn yours. You need to know that I've had one sexual encounter in my life; we both know how that ended for me."

A thunderbolt rolls through his chest, and I feel the shockwave of my words ripping free from his lungs.

Emotions coil through his expression, anger and tenderness and shock.

Logan lays entirely still, all except those piercing eyes that are hissing with desire across my face.

"Jesus, Ellie. I'm not sure I can respond in a way that you deserve. You let me be the first man to touch you goes to show a part of you trusted me from the get-go. Know this; I'm going to hunt after every bit of your trust, chase it down, and wear it out."

The unraveling thread that had drawn me to him when we'd met unspools a little more.

I still won't allow him to play me for a fool. No, I'll let him strip me bare and give me what I need, but I'll keep my guard up, shielding my heart.

"I don't want to own you, Ellie. I need to light you on fire the same way you do me. You don't have any idea how bad I want to kiss you right now, how much I ached to touch and feel and to erase every man before me out of your beautiful mind the night we met. Of course, that was before I knew no other man brought out your passion."

He slides his nose down mine, inhaling deep.

I swallow, my body aching for his touch.

I remember because I felt it. The energy that flung itself wildly through the air.

It's flinging now.

Chaotic.

Suddenly my bedroom shrinks. His scent. His warmth. His everything consumes me and overtakes my rationality and flings it into the frenzy that is Logan and me.

"I watched you dance before I approached you, the swing of your hips, the way those longs legs bent and stretched and this ass," His hands roam around my back, slip under my panties and squeeze.

"I had to have you. My dick had never been so hard in my life. It's that hard again. Tell me it's okay to spread your legs and dip my tongue inside of you? Tell me it's okay to drive you out of your mind. To erase your fear."

He's hard alright. I can feel it against me.

My heart thumps rapidly at the back of my throat, so violently that it's difficult to take a breath. I can already feel Logan's mouth on me, the way he'd pluck my desires out of me the same way he did weeks ago. God, those magic words spilling from his lips slice me to my core.

If Logan's eyes could get any darker, they do as they flicker back and forth between mine. The hypnotic vitality of them is rising in a force that dares me to challenge. He's caught me in his spell — a powerful vibration of want and need and lust quiver through me.

Logan is right; this attraction is unexplainable.

Shudders fly through my chest when his big hand palms my face, these are the same sensations that caused me to become wobbly on my feet when I met him.

Regretful stormy eyes fall on me as I press myself as close to him as I can get.

Pure dread threatens to terrorize me. I draw in a breath, gut-twisting in a slow, sinking realization that Shadow will slowly bleed the life out of me if he were to find me.

"You won't get anything from me until you tell me about

Shadow." I despise saying his name. Every time I do, I feel sick.

I study the man promising me so much, and all I can do is pray this dark knight I never thought I'd see again doesn't crush me under his boot.

A tic flows across the stern line of his jaw. "Wasn't planning on keeping him from you, Ellie. Shadow was busted for trying to sell coke to a cop. He's been in prison for years. He's getting out in a little less than six months. Once he's out, I won't stop looking for him the same way I won't stop until I find out who it was that sent someone to hurt you, and when I do, I will kill him and them with my bare hands. The same way I killed the man who attacked you. Shadow doesn't know about me and you, not yet anyway."

There's the explanation of his battered knuckles. More importantly, it explains why Shadow never came after me.

I drop my eyes closed, and the terror builds. So extreme and painful. Because even though the words didn't come out of Logan's mouth, there's no doubt in my mind Shadow will track me down.

It's coming. That violent storm I dreaded. I have less than a year before it strikes.

It's unfair too that Shadow was sent away for drugs and got nothing for violating me. For turning me into a shell of a woman and living in fear.

I loathe him more.

My entire body trembles as I blink away tears filled with fear. Not over Logan killing that awful man, because no one knows how Shadow is there one second and gone the next better than me.

He's dark and dreary and disturbing.

Sinister.

Memories hurl, too near, too much pain, and there are still questions rattling in my head. I want them to stop.

Logan will never erase what Shadow did to me, however, he can capture my unwelcoming fear.

"You killed that man for me? Are you after Shadow because of me or is there more?" The shift in his eyes, the muscles flexing in his jaw, tells me Logan has killed before without hesitation.

"I did and yes I've killed before. I want Shadow dead mostly because of what he did to you. When I told you I wasn't a good man, that's part of what I meant. I hate people who hurt the innocent and get away with it. Hate them about as much as I do the law that allows them to. Shadow got away with hurting you, Ellie. I can't in all good conscience allow him to get out and think he can come after you again. Told you I felt guilty and there's nothing I can do to give you back what he took. Killing him is all I got to free your mind. I won't let him anywhere near you. Trust me to protect you, please."

I swallow, letting the fact sink in that I not only went home with a feeling I'd seen Logan before but a man who kills. A man who probably has his connections with the mob, his associates of the law who would destroy the evidence against him if he were caught. Nevertheless, because of my past and how I want nothing more than Shadow to die, I don't care if he kills people who hurt others. Wrong or not, I don't, not after what I've gone through.

"That's easier said than done, Logan."

I take into consideration I would have never known about Shadow if I wouldn't have met Logan. I would have walked around with the hope I've clung to as if it were my lifeline to exist that Shadow forgot about me, and then he would have appeared, and God only knows what would have happened. Logan wanting to protect me doesn't ease the worry, but I'll take it.

"I can't begin to imagine your fear, and I don't expect you

not to worry. What I do want is for us to enjoy ourselves. I won't keep you in the dark when it comes to Shadow. I should have come forward, and there is no taking away my guilt. It was damn hard living in the same city and not seeking you out. There's nothing I can do about that now. Even if you never wanted to see me again, I'll continue to protect you until I kill that son of a bitch, and if anyone attempts to hurt you again, there will be consequences. I'm sorry I wasn't able to put a bullet through his brain before he ever laid a hand on you."

I draw in a deep breath, hoping when I let it out, it takes the fear with it. It doesn't. What it does is pull in a new kind of hope. Faith in a stranger that when the time comes, that maybe, just maybe Logan will kill the man who will forever live inside of me.

Six months isn't very long to pretend. As confusing, as fearful of what lays ahead. I have to go on. If I don't, I'll turn into the woman I was after. And she is one I never want to live with again.

Images of the months that followed swarm my thoughts. I swallow them down; I won't let them get to me, won't let them burn my brain with Shadow's pungent smell.

"I never knew you lived here." Sadness envelops me. If things were to work out between Logan and me, there's more life wasted that Shadow stole.

"Born and raised." A smile spreads to take up his entire face. It's quite possibly the most beautiful thing I'd ever seen.

I hate to break it, but there's something more I need to know before I beg Logan to kiss me.

"I trust you'll keep me safe, Logan. I do. Whitney? Where is she?"

His smile vanishes, replaced by a deep frown.

"I don't know where she is. I'll come up with a solution for her."

I lay there fighting a smile of my own as Logan tells me Whitney doesn't have a dime to her name and how Shadow lost everything.

"It wouldn't surprise me one bit if Whitney hasn't gotten her claws into some rich man. The woman is just like her mother. I'll keep you and those you love safe, Ellie. You won't know my men are around. You need to be smart, and so does your family. No more wandering around by yourself."

Menace and hate and assurance roll off Logan's words and I've never felt safer. Maybe it's because I've never had anyone who cared enough to want to protect me. I don't know what it is, the same as I don't understand why I need Logan to erase Shadow from my mind.

"I'm not a fragile, weak woman, at the moment, I feel powerless and shaken. I'm okay, Logan. Fair warning though, if you hurt me, I won't give you a second chance."

He doesn't respond before his hands let go of my ass and come up to frame my face again while he nudges my legs apart, gently guides me onto my back and takes my mouth.

Possessively—and my body responds to it, leaping farther ahead of my tumbling heart.

Desire swims through my blood.

His tongue brushes slowly across my lips, and my mouth spreads wide sucking his tongue until he takes over the kiss, tangling and twisting and gaining control with a pull that sends heat between my now spread legs.

My body is on fire. Sparking and ready to burst into flames.

I struggle with a rush of light-headedness that swirls through my entire body.

The fire inside of me rises, and I can only pray I'm not making the biggest mistake of my life by giving in to Logan Mitchell. Because if he hurts me in any way, I'll be nothing but a pile of ash.

CHAPTER 10

Logan

There have been very few times in my life when I allowed regret to dig deep. Today and every day from here on out will be one of them.

I'm a twisted prick — a liar who should be sitting right next to Satan himself. The second I released all the lies about hurting her. I wanted to take every one of them back and speak the truth. Couldn't get them to come out. So what the hell do I do? I keep tumbling and piling on lie after lie. Won't be long until I'm living in the shit I'm coating myself with.

But there are some dirty secrets a man needs to hold close to his chest, and the ones I'm clinging to will rip her open. Right now, I need to remind her to feel that draw, the pull, and attraction between us. To let loose and sweep the fright that has to be slipping through her strength because someday soon, I'm going to be kneeling at her feet and begging her to forgive me for doing her unjustifiably wrong.

Guarantee Ellie will never forgive me. Never give me a chance to explain, not after she made it clear not to lie to her again.

"The thought of me being the one to bring out the passionate woman in you has me being a desperate man. The things I need to do to you, sweetheart, are downright carnal. I need you to ride my face so I can eat your pussy until you come in my mouth."

Fuck the need and want. They are things that go hand in hand to me, and I want Ellie as much as I need air.

My body vibrates and shakes. This situation I've gotten myself into is going to end before I have the chance to prove she has everything I need and want in a woman. Everything my fucked up mind has stopped me from believing I deserve if I don't come clean.

The thing is, when I'm near her, looking into those eyes, I see a future with a happy ending, it makes it impossible to force the words out of my mouth. Can't blame myself when I laid next to Ellie for hours. That smooth as silk skin under the tips of my fingers a temptation and my conscious mind fighting against the swell of my cock to find the right way to tell her everything.

I'm manipulating her the only way I know how. Seducing her and when she finds out, it's going to devastate her.

Disgrace. A pig. A selfish son of a bitch.

I'm those and more.

Ellie's the kind of woman who makes a man think long and hard about what he'd do to keep her, and that's a big goddamn problem for me. Because if she keeps wedging farther under my skin, it won't be long until she's slithered into my heart, and in the end, when I do lose her, it'll smash mine as much as hers.

A gasp falls from her sweet mouth. There isn't anything I can do but breathe it in and take. Give her pleasure and watch her unravel.

The air grows heavy between us, and every second that ticks, the agony drains from her gorgeous face, leaving whatever hypnotic thing that drew us together in the first place.

It dangles close enough for me to brush my fingertips across, but it will always be out of my reach.

"I need you screaming my name because the only thing you're able to think about is my tongue between your legs sucking on your hard wet clit. You need me to find the spots on your body that set you aflame. You need me to touch your smooth skin, to run my hands up your thighs and spread you wide. You need my mouth on your overheated flesh, my tongue on your aching nipples, my lips on yours. You need my cock as much as I need to slip inside your slick wet pussy. You need to lose control as you did before."

Breaking in her body is the easy part of getting to the core of this woman because unlike most women I've fucked, Ellie's body doesn't lie.

She moans a yes and closes her eyes, my mind anticipating the things I could do to this woman, the way she's going to fall apart when I give her what she needs.

Fuck, I want to tie her up, spread her legs and ravish her.

I have one leg on the other side of hell anyway. May as well get what I can before the gates open wide.

Her soft whimpers of anticipation are my undoing. "You like it rough and so do I," I rumble against those fuck-able lips of hers. So fucking delicious that I can't wait for her to wrap them around my cock.

When my thumb brushes across the cut, her face curls against the light grip of my hand. Seeing that there makes me want to kill the man all over again. Only this time, I'd do it by beating the flesh off his bones.

I swallow, dive back in, and inhale her shaky little breaths. My lips pressing firmly against hers. Every time I taste her, I feel alive.

Unable to contain myself any longer, I slide one hand to

the back of her neck, keep my eyes open, and fuck her mouth.

Consuming as the world outside of her bedroom fades. I take what I want without guilt. Everything inside of me goes quiet. The only thing I hear is her moans. The only thing I feel is her tongue exploring my mouth.

She tastes like mine.

Strength and beauty and sunshine.

Her breath hitches when I unhook from her mouth and slide down her body and pitch onto my knees.

Gripping the silk of her panties by those curvy full hips that drive me out of my mind, I pull them down her legs, exposing the sweetest cunt I've seen and tasted.

I inhale. Her arousal is erotic and smells divine. Before tasting Ellie, it had been a long time since I ate pussy. Might have fucked women left and right. Always having my dick wrapped tightly but going down on one. Not a goddamn chance.

"Seeing you like this, breathless and tempting, body aching for more makes me lose my mind. I'm going to eat your pussy. I'm going to drive us both insane while I learn and teach and when I finally fuck you again, your build up will fucking explode."

The sound of her gasp goes straight to my cock.

All I see when I look up at her are darkened eyes, an enticing open mouth, and pink cheeks — hard nipples through the thin shirt covering up her full breasts. Everything I've dreamed, her face, her tight little body would express right before I seduced her is pouring out of her.

"Fucking beautiful."

All we do is stare at each other as my hands grip hold of her ankles. Her even allowing me to touch her is more than I could ask after what happened.

I'm not a believer that what I'm doing is going to erase

the years of pain she's lived. Fighting those demons that live in a beautiful soul I have no right to taint.

Her legs quiver from my touch. They shake the higher my dirty hands climb up her smooth skin. By the time I dip them underneath the hem of her shirt, pushing it high enough to get a glimpse of her tits, she's squirming. Her pulse is thrumming alongside the delicate slope of her neck.

Fuck, she has a nice rack. My cock needs in between those firm breasts.

"Jesus, Ellie." I inhale as I take a long look at her pretty pink pussy and take stock to memory the view of it neatly trimmed in my face, wetness leaking down her thighs. There's no darkness obscuring my perfect view like before when I carried her through my house.

Flawless.

Mine.

About came in my jeans when she said no one had been inside her. It pissed me off and had me grateful at the same damn time. My needy cock is begging to sink inside of her again. Every time I think of her from now on, I'll have a hard-on thinking of her glistening pussy wet only for me.

Christ, if and when I lose her, I'm going to suffer. I can already see it waiting to slither inside. That 'I told you so' sitting at the base of my ear.

Leaning in, I tunnel my shoulders between her thighs, spread her legs, my fingers kneading into her flesh, my tongue licks the line of her juices on her thighs straight to her folds. Fuck me. She tastes incredible. A whole lot of sin mixed with her sweetness.

She's full of desire, flames roaring inside and I'm the man who's going to burn while I push them out.

"Logan."

My name a croaky moan when I snag her clit between my teeth and clamp down. I run my tongue around the nub that's hard as a diamond, soothing it before nipping my way down to where I plunder my tongue in her dripping wet channel.

I shove it into her as far as it will go. Bury my face and lick, nip and fuck her with my tongue.

Greedy, that's what I am.

Gluttonous for punishment.

Looking back up, expressive turned-on eyes bore into mine. My view from below this woman on the edge of coming has to be one of the most erotically intimate moments I've ever experienced in my life.

Her breath clips and her eyes slam shut when I replace my mouth with my middle finger and thrust inside, curling at just the right angle, and wiggle the tip.

Fuck, I want inside her.

Slowly opening her lids, she begs just the way I want her to. "Logan, please, I need to come."

I lift my head to test her. Pushing that control, she doesn't want to give a little further my way.

"Trust me, Ellie, you'll come when I tell you to come. If you do, I'll stop, turn you over my knee and spank your ass."

"No, you won't. I want more." She whimpers, caught up in my trance.

"I love tasting you. Love your tight little body. Your spicy little sassy mouth is one of the sexiest things about you. It gets me hard knowing you challenge me."

I watch her expression, her lips forming an O. That head of hers with all that black hair shaking back and forth, eyes flaming with a plea she's not quite ready to spit out of that sharp mouth.

She's going to cave, but she's also going to be stubborn. Wouldn't want her any other way.

"You want me licking your pussy, don't you? You'd let me

take every single thing that I want and need right now, wouldn't you?"

"Yes. Don't think for a second I don't know what you're doing, Logan. I said I was inexperienced, didn't say I was a fool."

I lift a brow.

"You're a lot of things, but a fool you are not. This pussy though, it's greedy for my fingers, tongue, and cock. Push your shirt up farther and pinch your nipples. I need to see you playing with those perfect tits."

Her face flushes, and just like I'm controlling her body, Ellie unclenches those soft hands I want to be wrapped around my cock and pumping hard. She lifts her head, bunches up the shirt and yanks it over in a rush. Shaky palms cover her breasts and fingers tipped in a shade of light pink tweak the hardened nubs.

"You're a woman after my heart, aren't you? Harder, pinch them until you feel the pain mixed with the pleasure of my tongue."

I slide in another finger and increase my strokes, dipping my tongue right back in. Ellie's breathing builds, her back arching and legs squeezing around my head as I lick a lazy circle around her throbbing clit. Those little noises coming out of her mouth causes blood to blast straight to my cock.

A dazed headrush.

"Oh good God, please," she screams, lifts those lush hips and presses herself farther into my face.

"That's my girl; take what you need."

We stare at each other as I flick my tongue in and out, actions guaranteed to send this woman over the edge.

"This is perfect." I tug on her clit, it throbs against my tongue. "I dreamt about what you'd look like sprawled out in the light of day. Pink and tight. I wondered if you'd taste just as sweet as before. You taste even better. I have a feeling you will every time I bury my head in between these thighs. I want to eat you until you bend to my will. I want to lick, brand your skin with my teeth, and my hands. I want to protect you from the assholes who look at you wishing they could have one little sample of what you taste like. Hold on, sweetheart; I'm going to make sure you know who this pussy belongs to."

We hold one another's thundery eyes until she pinches hers closed.

"I get you don't want to give me control. I need you to open your eyes, Ellie. Don't ever close them when a part of me is inside you. Watching you fall apart is a necessity for me."

I flick my tongue over her clit.

In an instant, her eyes shoot open, and I feel her shattering.

Spasms start rocking through the nerves of her pussy. Her pleasure under my control, my demand.

Gathering and agonizingly beautiful to watch.

"That's it, Ellie, come for me, come screaming my name."

She coils her fingers into my hair, yanking hard, a scream ripping from her throat.

"Logan."

Hearing my name is a mind shattering sound.

Makes me hate it and love it at the same damn time.

I run my lips over her mound, across the tremors that fire under the soft, pale flesh of her stomach. Her skin is as smooth as velvet.

I want to indulge and touch every inch.

By the time Ellie is done riding on ecstasy, her breathing back under control, tiny whimpers fading into the air. I look deep into her eyes, and I see it there. The distrust, the way she shamefully let me control her.

"Don't; this is the beginning of you and me. Tomorrow,

let me show you a piece of my world that I've never shown another woman. Let me set you free in every way." I'd give her the moon if I could.

For a moment, her eyes squeeze close before she nods calmly.

I only hope that nod was her accepting the fate she's mine. I'll fight for her with everything within me.

Fighting and fucking. I've been doing both for a long damn time.

Have this feeling once Ellie knows everything, I'll be stopping one of them and diving right back into the other.

CHAPTER 11

Ellie

Curiosity. It got the best of me.

The destination my hands steered me to is bewitching. I am not afraid of being here. I am not frightened in the least if whoever had someone attack me is here and figuring out a way to do it again. I will come at them with both barrels loaded. However, the things I've seen are a mass confusion to my overthinking mind.

Logan sparks me. He's the match that started the flame. I felt nothing for so long, and suddenly, I feel everything all at once. So on a stupid whim, I came here.

"Do you have any questions?" the gorgeous woman who's been giving the grand tour of a place I never thought I'd step foot in asks. Her name left my thoughts the second she took me into the first room. I stood there unable to move as I watched two women and a man go at it. One woman rode his face, and another straddled his lap with her head thrown back in utter bliss. And they were doing it right along with many others — all in the same room.

The act itself didn't turn me on. The woman's face, as she

came, did. She either wanted what she was getting, or she's a damn good actress.

A warning bell bangs around in my head.

A different kind than the one when I first discovered who Logan is.

How could a woman like me ever be enough when Logan has all this?

"Where is the teaching area?" I'm priming myself for the one question I'll probably regret asking.

She bites her bottom lip, hesitating as if she's contemplating on whether to answer. Makes me wonder if somehow throughout our time together she found out who I am. It wouldn't surprise me one bit if she did, wasn't like I was paying her much attention anyway. Not with what was happening in every room she took me in.

"It's off limits unless you're a student."

"Oh, I'm taking it school is in session." Somehow I manage to get the words out around the blaze that licks around my throat.

"It is, but it's not Logan doing the teaching. He stopped quite a while ago." She's gazing at me understandingly now. Yup, she most definitely knows who I am. "Listen, I don't know what's going on between you and Logan, it's none of my business. I will say, he has never taken a liking to anyone the way he has you. I've worked here for five years and I've met a lot of people. Made some good friends and I've made enemies along the way. I also met my husband here. I fell for him hard and when he told me this wasn't for him, I made a decision and I chose him. Not once have I regretted it. Not once has he asked me to quit working here. It's all about choices and trust. Wait in here; I'll grab you a bottle of water."

This is most definitely not my thing, and she isn't

bringing me water either. I'd dare to guess it won't be long before Logan is barging through the door.

"Thank you."

Someone once said a curious mind is the most powerful thing a person owns. I never gave that much thought until mine got the best of me and I decided to come to this club thinking it would be the best way to see this side of Logan with my own eyes. After the things I saw people doing in front of others, I firmly believe a person's body is more powerful than anything else. It's a weapon for seduction.

And I have no idea how to seduce a man.

I lean up against the glass as she shuts the door, barely able to breathe, feeling the cold, slimy fingers of men and women who watched me with hawk-like eyes when I stepped through the entrance of Behind Closed Doors. Women and men, both sex-driven eyed me as if they'd take the chance to meet every one of my desires. They all gawked at me like I was fresh meat and they couldn't wait to take a bite. I can still feel them crawling up my spine and squeezing my neck with all the strength they had.

Ruthless and savage.

On legs barely able to hold me up, I nearly jump out of my skin, a little squeal breaking free as I turn around, cutting my unraveling mind from the door to the noise coming from behind me.

I gasp, and my eyes bug when I realize my little tour hostess has shut me in one of the private rooms she pointed out earlier. "Why in God's name would she put me in the line of a room full of people doing things I will never be able to erase?"

My gaze remains on the couples sprinkled just beyond my reach. The view from here is like standing right in front of them. I can make out what everyone on the other side of the room is doing in their cushy little booths. I can see some of the action on the beds lining both sides of the wall.

They are kinkily fucking and sucking and enjoying themselves.

Just like every other fancy nightclub I've been to, Behind Closed Doors is as reverberating and elegant as the rest. Marble bars, bright lights, leather couches, booths set under a soft sensual glow of dim lights, and the smell of a night filled with dirty sex in the air — drinks delivered by women wearing less than nothing. Men and women are grinding against one another on the dance floor to music with a heavy thumping sexual beat that does its job by hitting you in the middle of your legs.

This club is gorgeous on the inside, three floors in a renovated Plantation situated on The West Bank of The Mississippi River. There are even cabins that are rented out by the day, the week, the weekend, for members to host private parties.

I can't even imagine what goes on inside of them.

The spacious room in front of me is decorated in oldschool southern charm, and the paintings on the walls are eye-catching. Women in the throes of ecstasy as they take on two men. Guys with their heads buried between one woman's legs while another sits on his cock — men with men. Women with women and people are standing in the shadows watching. All of them calling out as if they'd seen and held the millions of sex acts I'd imagine performed inside this building, and everywhere you look the standard rule of no means no is plastered in bright neon colors.

And there are cameras everywhere. Noticing them has me keeping my eye on the door through the window expecting Logan to come barreling through and demand me to leave. He could try. I have every right to witness with my own eyes what goes on in here. After all, he flung me in it without telling me.

"You told him you didn't want to know about this club, Ellie." I whisper.

The thing is, all I have left to give is my heart. I won't give it to anyone I don't believe will cherish it. It's silly to think Logan wants it when we barely know each other, and I'm far from ready to give it away. Still, I had to see this part of Logan's life.

From what I've seen and what is happening at the moment, I'm not as prepared for this as much as I convinced myself I was, much like the man who drew me into wanting to get to know him.

A chain that looped around my ankle and tugged me straight toward him.

While this looks like a typical night club, it's anything but, it's exactly what Eric said it was. A place where sexual fantasies come to life.

I tremble when I see a man shove his hand up a woman's shirt on the dance floor and another man lifts her skirt, his fingers dive into the front of her panties as she grinds her ass into the man behind her, throws her head back onto his shoulder and the man in front of her takes her mouth.

It's been less than an hour since I paid the hefty cover charge, signed an NDA, gave up my phone and license, and now I stand here watching people get out of their seats with multiple partners and head toward the exit. There are men with arms wrapped around two women, there are three of the same sex, as well as couples, and my guess is once they've reached the point of wanting sex and they don't want an audience that's when they leave this giant orgy party for privacy.

Sex and lust and a creative sexual mind, it's everywhere, but none of what goes on here is for me unless it was done in private between a man and me. Not just any man, the very man who owns this place. The very man who turns me on as I watch.

A shudder rolls through every inch of my body, and a shaky breath leaves my lungs as I recognize a few male celebrities as well as a highly known news reporter fucking with reckless abandon. I whimper around the knot of desire that sticks in my throat. Nerves of insecurity only magnifying the sensation as I watch a woman place her hands on a man's shoulders and push him down on one of the many beds lining the far wall of the room. She straddles him with her back to his chest and swivels her hips before taking hold of him and guiding his dick inside of her.

And she rides him.

Fast and hard.

A gasp tears from my lungs, and my already thrumming sex shoots heat straight down my legs. My toes curl in my sky-high heels.

I'm flushed. I'm fevered. I'm burning up.

She's in the driver's seat.

Oh, God. Is that what Logan meant about me driving?

It can't be, can it?

I'd wreck us if it is because I have no idea what I'm doing when it comes to sex. I'm surprised Logan even wants me again. He guided us through everything that night. Took what he wanted and gave in return.

I'm not enough for Logan Mitchell.

I scream when the door swings open and closes with a loud slam.

Through the window, I catch Logan slowly moving his way toward me. The sight of him increases the throbbing between my legs. My mouth waters, and my stomach clenches.

This time he's caught off guard. But this is different. He knows it is too.

That need closes in on us. The one whenever we're around one another is so powerful it shouldn't exist.

A disorder of uncertainty is running through him. I can feel those eyes of his burning into me from behind as if he's wondering why I'm here and what he's going to do about it.

Relieve me of my ache, please.

"I would have gladly brought you here if you had asked. Now that you are, whatever should I do with you, Ellie? Give you what you need? Take what I want? Fuck you until you promise to never step foot in here again? Have you spread those thighs and finger yourself while I slide my cock between your lush tits? What will it be?"

Logan moves forward like a cat sneaking up on a trapped little mouse. Every step sends my heart into a frenzy. It bounces off one side of my ribcage to the other, back and forth until I can barely breathe.

I'm so lost in my mind that by the time he plasters his chest to my back, slips a hand around my stomach, and tugs me firmly against his hard chest, his head dipping down to rest his chin on top of my head, I can't think past him relieving me before I do it myself.

Why does it become so much harder to think as soon as Logan comes anywhere near me?

Want and need.

They embed in my brain.

"You were turned on before you saw me. Your body and those deep blue eyes give you away, Ellie. It's a known fact how, we, as creatures act when we want sex. Our bodies break out in a sweat, our pupils dilate, we shake, we shiver, and we unravel. Men get painfully hard, and women get rousingly wet. I bet if I touched you, you'd be dripping. Me,

I'm hard as stone. My balls are tight, and I'm in agony to hike up your skirt and fuck you so hard. But..."

Logan's muscles relax except his rock-hard cock probing into my back while I stand, pressing my thighs together as if doing so would relieve the throb that increased the second he touched me.

I try to unthaw my tongue that's suddenly frozen to the roof of my mouth. I'm so far out of my comfort zone. A willing hostage to this man who was puppeteering me when I don't want anyone controlling my strings.

But this was Logan. A teacher, and he's going to devour me.

An easy-going gush of air leaves him, and every bit of tension releases from his magnetic body. It becomes replaced with needy pants heaving with control and certainty.

"But what?" I manage to say through a puff of headiness.

"You need to be taught a lesson about the woman you are to me, Ellie. My pulse kicked up the minute I saw you. Those long legs of yours are the only ones I want to be wrapped around me. Your laugh, your mouth that says so much but at the same time holds things in; I want to kiss and lick and coax every word out of it, even if you're telling me off. Your inexperience, do you have any idea what that does to me? It makes me rock-fucking-hard. You don't need to be taught a thing, Ellie. It's me who's the student here. It's me who's not enough, and do you know why?"

I inhale a sharp breath, so close to unraveling, my head spins.

"Because I don't want this kind of life anymore, Ellie. Why would I, when the most fascinating woman I've ever met wants me in spite of the man I was. Don't doubt yourself when it comes to you not being enough for me again. We've only begun, Ellie. There is so much we have to learn about one another. I can't wait to crawl inside your mind. I look forward to holding your hand. I want simple; I want to talk to you, to breathe you in. I want everything you have to give. I have one question, and if you answer it correctly, we'll both pass."

Slowly, he rotates me so I face him, which makes the ache ten times worse. Because that connection I don't understand, it bangs like a high-pitched cymbal in the space between us. It triples when he runs his hand down my arm, grabs hold of it and lifts, kissing my knuckles once again — keeping his hot mouth on my skin for several beats before dropping his forehead to mine.

Our bodies are so close; I can feel every fitful beat of his heart. I can almost hear the rush of the blood pumping through his veins. Could taste the desire that comes off his skin.

We are both panting.

"What is it you want from me, Ellie?"

Reality sluggishly seeps back into my mind, and I fight with what to say.

"I, I want to be enough for you. I want the same things you do. I want you to touch me, feel me. I want you to need me as much as I do you. I want safety. I want a life. I want all of you too."

"Passed with flying colors. However, I haven't been given a chance to prove myself out of the bedroom yet. We started off backward. It doesn't mean we can't continue and let our chemistry fly through the roof. There are circumstances where actions are needed as much as words, Ellie. Tomorrow I'll give you proof of the kind of man I am. Tonight, I want you to guide me. Tell me what you crave. I want to find the spots on you that set you aflame. I never wanted or needed to be with a woman the way I do you."

His words grip hold of my chest, his lips start doing that

little knowing quirky lift at the corners just begging me to try and deny.

Impossible.

"I want you to make me fall apart."

"Oh, I will. You need extra credit first, Ellie. An essay that I'll gladly give. You need to know that one night with you made me see past the walls of this place. How I could turn my life around and at the same time I could bring more pleasure to you than you've dreamed. You are enough for me; want to know why?"

He nips at my jaw, hands sliding to my ass where he shoves my skirt up and palms the cheeks.

"Yes." My voice is shaky from lust.

"You are all that I see. Your outside beauty shines from within, your heart sings. You are kind, but you want to be bad. You are strong; you are a light that blinds me. I might not know you, but I damn sure know a good woman who wants to be wicked in the bedroom and I'm a lucky man knowing it's me you desire." He groans as he cups my ass, squeezing hard. I wouldn't be surprised if he leaves a mark; I welcome the fingerprints.

"Oh, God. What are you doing to me?"

Lust must play out across my features for a moment before his smile turns wicked, and he presses his hardness into my belly.

I knew he was a master at seduction.

"Please, Logan. I need—"

"To come," he hoarsely finishes for me.

"Yes. I need you to make me come."

"Fuck. Not sure what sounds sexier, you panting my name or asking me to make you come."

Both, I think to myself.

His big hands scorch my skin as they slide up my sides, stopping to rest on my cheeks.

Logan is a toucher, he's intense and strikes you with a deep sense of reality with both his words and his touch.

Dark eyes show a glimpse of so much pleasure that I feel my wetness soak my panties.

"Give me your mouth. I want to touch your skin, kiss your lips, and taste you. You are the sweetest, sexiest addiction I've ever had."

CHAPTER 12

Logan

A silent spell falls upon us. I stare at her while those eyes I could watch all day are full of so much yearning it wrecks me.

Her face is a vision of innocence, purity, and lust. It's a combination of an angel with a side dish of sin. When our eyes collide—and goddamn, do they ever—it's like lightning striking an electrical tower. Sparks fly all around. Never in my life have I felt a jolt of electricity hit me just from looking into a woman's eyes.

It powers right through my veins.

Need.

It licks a trail up my dick.

I want to go animalistic on her. Push her as far as she'll let me. I also want to discover everything that turns her on. What parts of her skin will make her squirm with the touch of a finger. Make her beg with my tongue — pant, and scream when I slide into her. I want to kiss her skin lightly, roughly. I want to mark her until she's dripping with me. I want to watch her face as she comes so I can brand it into my memory until I erase any remaining shred of doubt.

The minute Seth called to tell me Ellie was here, and I strolled through our office door like a man gone wild; he was about two seconds from having his fingers broken from where he firmly wrapped a hand around my forearm because I needed to maim someone. Preferably myself for expecting this woman with a mind as sharp as a tack would not want to know about this place once she thought about it.

This place, my life, the women, they were a means to make money for me. Sure, I got off. Immense pleasure? Not even close to the kind Ellie brings out and we haven't even begun to explore.

I'm not quite sure what Ellie is doing here, let alone trying to prove by thinking she isn't enough. If I knew her better, she'd be over my knee for pulling a reckless stunt like this. Newbie night isn't the best night for someone who has no desire to dip into this lifestyle. It's the worst night of the month. The kink level is higher than most nights because the women are up for anything and men outnumber them.

I spotted her straight away when I glanced at the wall full of monitors and watched closely as she gazed out the one-way mirrored window.

All that hair pulled up in a sleek, shiny ponytail. Her low dipped shirt leaving little to the imagination of what laid underneath. And, Christ, I about lost it when I noticed her long legs were bare. My eyes traveled up those legs, dick growing when I noticed she had on a black leather skirt that hugged the plump curves of her juicy ass. Those big blue pools of hers were full of lust as she watched an orgy.

I couldn't take my eyes off of her.

Rapt.

Her exquisite beauty reduced me to nothing.

Christ, I wanted to take her right where she stood as I firmly gripped hold of those curvaceous hips, bent her over the couch in the corner of the room and pushed her short skirt up and over her ass. Fuck her until she promised never to come here again.

"Logan, please." Her request is a needing plea.

She smiles. It's insecure. Ellie is out of her mind if she believes she isn't enough. Suppose I'm the guy to give her a lesson in assurance even though the one doing the teaching is her.

Her palm touches my cheek. Delicate finger running back and forth over my stubble. It's soft, tender and warm like her lips. It feels unbelievably good when she touches me. I can't wait until she wraps those fingers around my dick and jacks me off.

When she begs with those bright blue eyes that do me in every time, her mouth parting, I lower my head and take.

I devour her sensual mouth. She gives back in return.

I kiss her until she melts into me. Without breaking apart, I hoist her up, step backward, her arms going around my neck, legs dangling in the air until I plant us on the couch, positioning those long toned legs around me.

"You are enough for me. Get that through your head. I would never, nor do I want to touch another woman ever again. You either take my word for it, or you don't. The choice is yours, just like giving me a chance is yours," I whisper into her mouth, gulping down her panting breaths; those noises are as real as the pulse of this woman in my veins.

I've told many lies while being with a woman; they flew freely from my tongue. With Ellie, I'm clear, focused, and everything I say to her doesn't even begin to soak up the truth of what I see when I look at her.

She's a gift I don't want to return. One if I could, I'd open every day for the rest of my life.

There's no turning back for me after her.

Ellie's feet are on the gas, and I'll go at her pace getting to know her, but the rush, the need to be inside her won't slow down.

With Ellie, I forget. With her, I can be me, and that is the best thing this woman can give me. Her body is a bonus.

I wait for a sassy comeback; when none comes, I run my hands up her naked thighs, break away from her mouth and stare into her out-of-focus and heated eyes, testing my resolve not to fuck her right here and now. I might ease the ache between her legs, but I will never taint her sweet body by fucking her here.

"I'm sorry, I won't doubt myself again," she words softly.

Jesus, this woman, she's going to do me in. So pure, I could get drunk on it.

"Once again, I'm the one who should be sorry, Ellie. I should have never left this part of my life wide open. I should have known you wouldn't leave it alone. It's done. The door to this life is closed. I have to work in the office, but that's all I'll be doing when I'm here."

That's the truth. The idea of another woman touching me makes me as nauseous as thinking about a man touching Ellie.

My lies and betrayal, they hang over my head.

A predatory reminder that they could drop and rip us in two at any given time.

Doesn't stop me once again from taking a little more of this woman, while allowing her to unwilling thief a little more of me.

I run my hands up her thighs, under her skirt, and lightly across her soaking silk panties, where I seek the tiny bud, give it a pinch and caress the line of her slit.

Damn, is she drenched.

My tongue darts out to sweep across her lips and before I have the chance to tease, I begin sucking down her every exhale in a deep kiss as she grinds into my hand. Her glazed-over eyes roll into the back of her head as she seeks out what she needs.

"Jacked off at least a dozen times these past few weeks thinking about this pussy," I mumble into her mouth before diving back in.

My mouth moves from hers to that elegant neck, exploring and nipping as I go. By the time I get to the shell of her ear, she's panting and moaning and squirming above me, right where she belongs. "You taste so good. Smell divine and edible. My mouth waters thinking about your pussy. It's the sweetest flavor ever to coat my tongue." Another truth, regardless if it's meant to reaffirm her confidence.

"And this mouth of yours." I skim back down her neck, take her mouth once again and deepen our kiss that turns into a wild frenzy. "I can't wait to have it wrapped around me. Can't wait for more sass so I have an excuse to kiss you." I lick every corner, every crevice in the well of her delicious mouth and sweep my tongue across her straight white teeth.

"Your mind is in chaos, and I want to crawl inside and straighten it out. I want your heart as much as your body, and I'll fight dog dirty to get every bit of you there is to give."

It doesn't take but a second before I'm craving to make her come. A groan deep in the confines of my throat erupts when I stroke her clit, push her panties aside and plunge a finger inside of her heat.

Warm and tight.

I tease her clit, apply pressure with my thumb around the sensitive nub. She huffs out a breath and lifts her hips.

I don't need to teach this woman a damn thing. She's a natural at seduction without even knowing it.

She's the teacher, the driver, and I'm the asshole who will be asked to get out long before we reach a destination.

I must be insane. Either that or desperate to have a bit of good in my life before everything turns to shit.

I bite her bottom lip, then skim my mouth down her neck, planting kisses everywhere. She squirms, pants. Her body is coming alive, turning to perfection in the palm of my hands.

"You feel me touching you, kissing you? This silky, flawless skin is perfection." For the life of me, I'll never understand how she could ever doubt herself.

"Yes, I feel and hear."

Christ, her voice is throaty and husky; there's not a fake thing about it.

Just like her.

"You better."

If it's the last thing I do before she kicks me out of her life is to unbend her lack of thinking she isn't enough. The more I think about anyone else seeing her breasts, feeling the warm well of her pussy, the more jealous I get. Can't even stomach the idea.

I palm her ass with my free hand, squeeze and repeat.

While my finger drives in and out of her pussy, my mouth seeks out one of her nipples and I latch my teeth onto it through her shirt and bra, pulling, tugging from gentle to hard.

Her arousal fills the air. That sweet addiction powers my finger to drive faster. She moans, arches her back enough to plant her tits in my face. I bite down gently as she gives me her orgasm by coming undone with an easy-going sigh.

A few minutes later, she pulls in a deep breath as I tuck her to my side and walk her through the club, a fret of nervous tension rolls down her spine until I open her car door and tuck her safely inside.

And as I follow her home in the deep dark of night with the glow of the city around me, I know I flunked, and she passed the class on her first try.

I failed every year that I didn't make Ellie mine.

CHAPTER 13

Ellie

"How's your eye? Have you iced it? Do you need anything?" Renita's concerned voice blares through the speakerphone as I run my hands over the smooth black wrapping paper of a box that was delivered to me a few minutes ago.

At first, due to what happened, it frightened me, but when the delivery man told me he had strict orders to let me know it was from Logan, a thrill rushed through my chest and smacked into my breastbone.

The man is going to unbalance me by coming at me in ways impossible to ignore — the same way he's done with every encounter.

Those eyes of his pulling me in as he steals another piece of me, washing away my fear, my panic, my doubt. All the while slipping a little farther in.

My body is waking up, and my mind is spinning in a deep sea of emotion—need and hunger and getting to know a man I don't come close to understanding.

I told myself I would never fall helpless to a man. Still,

Logan makes my body ache with a need that makes my pulse run wild.

I pick the box up, my shaky fingers slipping under the tape and tearing off the paper. Pushing open the flaps, I gasp and pull out a black motorcycle helmet with a colorful feather painted on the side.

"That's perfect for you," Norah whispers.

A gift such as this should sadden me. For some reason, it doesn't. It pulls a smile clear across my face and stalls my breath.

The force of Logan is coming on strong, and if I don't come to my senses, he's going to wreck and rule me completely.

Sweep me into the clouds to where I'll never touch solid ground.

I need to remember it's my heart that's on the line when it comes to this man.

"I agree." I hesitate before saying more, remembering Renita is on the phone, and even though she can't see me, I'm here worrying my lip with my teeth.

"I'm fine, Renita."

It's been less than eight hours since I made her aware of what happened and she's called three times. Renita is none too happy with me at the moment. I told her everything about Logan knowing Shadow. I couldn't keep it from her anymore. She has the right to know.

It was pointless to argue when she has her rights; our conversation ended with her telling me under no circumstances pick Logan apart. Renita might be the type of mother who let go of her apron strings when us girls moved out, but she'll always be the momma bear who protects her babies.

I suppose I'd be too.

"Okay. You know where I'll be if you need me. My shotgun is loaded. This mother hen isn't afraid to use it."

Typically, her comment would be a joke. It's not. Knowing Renita, she does have it loaded.

"I know you would, Renita."

"She's lying; I punched her because Logan asked her out and they are finally going on a date. He sent her a motorcycle helmet, Mom. And this date is why she splurged on a pair of sexy black motorcycle boots. Did you wax the goods too?"

I shoot Norah a dirty look; I didn't do that. I dragged the boots out of the back of my closet, dusted them off not having any idea Logan was taking me for a ride.

I still don't, but if this helmet is a hint, then I've dressed right.

"Thank you," I mouth. Knowing Norah is trying to lift the tension off of Renita's shoulders. I appreciate her for it, but she should know her mother won't rest until she sees Logan with her own eyes.

"Renita, do you remember the time you wished you only had one daughter, and her name was Ellie Mae? I'm not asking for a friend," I joke, sliding right back into the teasing banter I've missed between the three of us.

"I do. You were always my favorite; don't tell what's-her-face. She's always been the trouble maker of my girls." My entire body shakes as a laugh sparks up from deep down. There's the Renita I know.

"Oh, the two of you are so hilarious. As you can hear, your favorite daughter is fine, Mom. I'll see you tomorrow." I wait for Norah to disconnect before wiping the smile off my face and addressing her question, which I should ignore, just like everything else with my busy body best friend, she'll ask about down below again if I don't answer.

"Trust me; everything is fine down there. Maybe you should start worrying about yourself. You haven't dated in a while."

I wad up and toss the wrapping paper in her direction,

not bothering to remind her I've never had a reason or the desire to wax. Although I do keep myself neat and trimmed.

"I don't know. Tired of settling, I guess. Besides, I'm going to kick back and live a little through you."

"Well, you might be kicking back until you shrivel."

"No, you'll cave and spill once Logan gets his hands on you again."

The thought of Logan's hands on me again sends a buzz through my body. The rational side of me, the one who woke up with a slight tinge of regret has been trying to push her way through most of the day.

I've shoved her ugly voice away.

I'd much rather take a ride on the wild side with the Devil. When I'm with Logan, I feel safe, as if nothing or no one can touch me. It's ridiculous, but the thought, plus him letting me know last night before he left he has someone protecting me, just in case, is what's going to get me through the next month without worry.

Logan Mitchell is opening my eyes, and in return, I want to peel away his layers, to flick through every single one until I get to the surface. To hide away underneath, and burrow as deep as I can get into that clarity of danger and dark.

Ignoring the smirk on Norah's face, I roll my eyes and make my way toward the opposite end of the counter to close the register.

This banter between Norah and me is good; she's been riding my ass since the attack on why Logan's brother just happened to be in our neighborhood, nearly working me into a frenzy of tattered nerves. I must have had a dozen texts last night from her asking me where the hell I was.

I'm not much of a liar. Honesty is essential to me, so I finally broke down and told Norah the truth. We fell asleep in my bed, woke up and had breakfast, laughed and kept the worry out of our conversation. Today has been a great day, and I hope tomorrow is even better.

"Even with what happened to you, there's a glow on your face. Did you have sex last night and not tell me?"

Visions blaze.

Logan between my legs.

Big and self-confident and so damn irresistible.

"No. I'm not sleeping with him. Not tonight anyway."

I can't help it; the apex between my thighs starts to ache.

"Okay, whatever you say, my sweet turned naughty best friend. That part about not sleeping with him, you might need to talk with your vagina. I'm pretty sure she won't agree."

"What? Why?"

A deep sigh leaves her mouth, and I follow her gaze to where a man turns a few female passerby's heads as he swings one long black jean covered leg over a motorcycle in front of the store and leans against it.

Smooth big arms hang at his sides. His colorful sleeve of leaf and vine tattoos swirl down one arm, thick thighed legs overlap at the ankles, and a heated gaze is locking on mine through the clear shield of his helmet for a moment before he unhooks it, tugs it off his head and shakes the dark locks of his hair.

Oh. My. God.

"Holy shit. I'm in trouble. Deep dark water kind of trouble."

The man is turning me inside out with his hot as fuck persuasion and oozing dominance. He's caring and protective too. I don't know what part of Logan is more concerning to me; the only thing I know is seeing him standing there is taking my breath away.

He's going to do more than muddle my head in the clouds; he's going to leave me floating on them.

And, wrong or right, I want him too.

One corner of Logan's mouth curls up, and it's like the clouds drop low, the humidity rises right before a thunderstorm.

Heat.

It radiates off that muscular body from where he stands and the intensity of it blows right at me.

Suggestive and assured.

My heart bounces and thumps.

"Yeah, you are. Something tells me that gorgeous hunk won't let you drown."

No, he won't. I'm pretty sure I'll go under several times from the intensity dripping off him like a sudden crashing wave, an undertow that will snatch me right off my feet.

If I'm not careful, I won't resurface.

I stumble a little when he runs a big hand through the messy strands of his hair, soft affection regarding me. Between the way he fucked me the night we met, compared to the other night in my bed, last night and right now, it leaves me realizing there are many layers to his personality, and without a doubt, it'll be hard deciding which one I like best.

A full smile spreads across Logan's face. I love it when the man smiles. This one hits me in the spot that aches, making me wet. Because this man, the one who promised me a piece of his world last night, is here to pick me up on a motorcycle.

I can already feel the wind whipping through my hair.

Frantically, I glance back at Norah, who is smiling at me. Her happy expression is igniting the kick inside of being reckless and free as I cling onto the hard planes of Logan's abs. I can feel the rumble of the bike under my ass, legs spread and tingling from being pressed close to the man whose clear intentions are the same as mine. To peel back layers and discover the real me.

Logan is going to stretch me taut and tight while winding my senses.

Seeing him standing there with a cocky grin on his face; I want never to remind myself he's dark, deadly, and dangerous.

God, the man has killer eyes to go along with his killer hands, intimidating body, and a dirty mouth.

Eagerness strikes my blood, and a flame hits the tip of my toes. I have it bad for a man that is too much for a woman like me to handle.

"I expect you to have a good long and hard ride, lady. I'll lock the doors."

Straightening myself up, I rush toward the door with my helmet in hand. I'm not about to comment on Norah's innuendo right now. Not when I haven't been on the back of a motorcycle since my father died.

"Okay." My word comes out breathless.

I take Logan in as I pull open the door, collecting his every feature, and for heaven's sake, I didn't think it was possible for him to be more beautiful, but he is.

He's danger and disorder.

Risky.

Intense.

Passion.

Authority and power a threat I don't want to ignore burning from his perfect body. I feel the undeniable electricity that sizzles between Logan and me with every small step I take.

A live wire is tugging us together. It's the most active thing I've felt in my life.

"Hi, thank you for the helmet."

The veins in his jaw twitch, but it's the way he responds when I get within hands reach that spreads a tremor beneath my skin.

Logan runs the tip of his index finger down my neck, pausing above the pulse that is fluttering out of control. A knowing gleam of satisfaction flits in his eyes.

"It picked up speed the minute you saw me, didn't it?"

"Don't be a smug asshole, Mr. Mitchell."

"Mr. Mitchell?"

"Shut up, Logan."

He throws his head back and laughs — all the while keeping his finger on my frazzled pulse.

I feel as if parts of me are detaching—my body, mind, and soul thrash through my insides from his gentle touch.

"You're welcome. I hope it fits. Have you been on a bike before?"

Fond memories lick at my skin. The excitement in my dad's voice when he'd holler up the stairs for me to grab my helmet because he wanted to go for a ride. The giggles coming out of my mouth and the way my stomach would twirl when he'd let me sit in front and help me steer until we reached the end of our drive.

Some of the fondest memories of my life and Logan unknowingly is given a piece of them back to me.

"Yes, it's been a while." Sadness swells, I push it back. Tonight isn't the night to think about the sorrow and grief that's been my life.

The smirk on his face mixed with a different gleam in his eyes tells me tonight isn't about the things he wants to do to me; it's about letting go, about simply being him and me. To trust and leap a little farther together.

He's looking at me as if he's reaching into my chest, tugging on my heartstrings, and pulling me toward him.

I don't know what is happening. It's frightening, and I need to keep reminding myself it's alright to give in to desire, to let Logan give what my body desperately needs, but also cling tightly to the parts of me I won't give freely.

Complete trust and my heart.

"You are naturally beautiful, Ellie. I loved the makeup last night, love this carefree look much better. There's nothing fake about you, is there?" His words sweep over my skin like the feather on my helmet.

A soft caress.

"No. I was taught to be who I am. If others don't like it, they can go fuck themselves." My mother's words.

Logan tilts his head. I swear I can see his pulse quicken in the veins in his neck. There's amusement in his expression. Whatever it is about him that has me drawn to him, it's a damn magnetic force, and I cannot seem to pull away.

A lump grows heavy in my chest, making it hard to breathe. I have never felt so unsure of the woman inside of me until him.

It's terrifying.

He leans in, fingers winding gently around my throat and runs his nose up the side of my neck, nuzzling his face into my hair.

Twice he inhales and exhales, sending whispers of his breath into the shell of my ear.

I tingle and spasm in a safe and arousing way.

My body fevers. I tingle everywhere. My nipples harden underneath my bra — sweat forms in between my breasts.

Heavy air whooshes out of my lungs. I take a step back only to have him run a devious pair of darkened eyes up and down my body, pausing at my black leather flat knee-high boots before slowly climbing back up to land on my face.

"I agree. I must add though, everything you wear, I want to peel off. You drive me so fucking crazy. I'm desperate to lean you back and fuck you on my bike."

God help me before he steals what little bit of control I have left.

I tremble, flailing to stay afloat, as his words rush through my veins at a rapid pace.

"I've been waiting all day for this mouth."

My body snaps to attention, desire like I've never felt before, eases throughout me as he spins us around, sets me on the seat of his bike with a thud, his hands fist my hair, hauling me forward, and his mouth closes aggressively over mine.

A moan leaks past my lips, my legs helplessly dangling at either side of him, while his lips drive me insane.

Gentle Logan is gone as he nips and bites. Stroking and taking complete authority of the rims of my mouth before he dips his tongue inside.

My starving body craves his kisses. Every single one has a raw intensity filled with yearning exchanged in the mixture of our billowing breaths.

"Let's see if this fits."

I surrender myself as he places the helmet on my head, and positions me how he wants me. All the while, knowing I have protection from Logan, but there's no one to save me from him.

CHAPTER 14

Logan

"No matter what happens between you and Ellie, you better not go back to the life you no longer belong to."

I grit my teeth, wishing I could go back in time so I could have made Ellie mine. Life would have been an entirely different road — one with fewer bumps, and one that wasn't leading me straight to hell.

A smooth road like the one Ellie and I rode on last night. Hours we spent on my bike, our thoughts to ourselves. Freedom in the wind. Her heartbeat increasing against my back when we take a sharp turn, her warmth all around me.

"Think I told you, I'm over that life, Gabe."

Gabriel Ricci took my brothers and me in after our parents died. He and his wife, Lena, God rest her soul, were close friends with my parents. The man is one loyal motherfucker and one of the few men I know who held true to his marriage vows by not cheating on his wife.

They fought tooth and nail to keep our mother from fucking up after our father died. Had her in and out of rehab, they did everything they could, and still, it wasn't enough to make her care.

On top of that, they managed the business the best they could. They are the sole reason why it didn't go in the red. And even though they hated that the three of us dug our heels in, they left the choice up to us and supported our decision.

After the three of us moved in with them, that's when we found out Gabe was mafia. The younger brother to Lazaro Ricci. The boss of The Italian-American crime family. Long story short. Lazaro and Gabe are the reason people don't mess with my brothers and me. They know we are under their protection. But, just as stupid is as stupid does, Shadow crossed that line when he attacked Ellie. Lazaro was all in on paying whatever it costs to have someone yank out Shadow's jugular while he did his time. Wish now like the night I killed the man who attacked Ellie; I would have taken him up, if I did, life would be a hell of a lot easier for me and a certain blue-eyed, black haired beauty.

"I sure the fuck hope so. There isn't anything better than a good woman standing by your side."

Fuck.

His words are a punch to the gut. Pretty sure he meant them to be.

"It wasn't hard to find Whitney. At the moment, she's with Ramon Cadena in Paris. Word has it they'll be heading to his summer home in Baton Rouge. I can't get inside Ramon's palace without talking to Lazaro, and I sure as shit ain't flying across the ocean to get the bitch. Give me a few weeks, and we'll have her out on her ass. Ramon cares more about having peace than he does about Whitney. He'd shoot her in the back of the head if I asked."

No wonder she hasn't tried blackmailing me. Bitch is

working her sloppy self on someone else like I thought. Someone with enough power to destroy me.

A thousand warnings shout in my head. Cadena is the head of the Mexican Cartel. He might make his millions by dealing drugs, that doesn't mean he can't be persuaded to step on our toes, especially if he gets hold of the many names to bribe me with.

This is why my brothers and I have men watching us all the time because every greedy man wants to rule the sex world. Those bloodthirsty assholes have no idea how to run a business as deep as ours, let alone treat the women who would work for them. Been down that road before, and it's one of many reasons why I want Shadow dead.

"Let's hope you're right."

"I give you my word I am. Ramon is an ally, not an enemy. Whitney fucked up. It's the mistake we needed. With that said, I'm ruling Whitney out as a suspect. She hasn't left Ramon's place in weeks. I think we need to look in our neck of the world."

In spite of the shit going down, a smile tugs at my mouth. Gabe built a house across the street from Lane shortly after my niece was born to help out. He's been on some long ass fishing trip in Canada for months. Left when I called him to inform him someone hurt Ellie. He was due back next week.

"Does this mean you're coming home?"

"Yeah, son, I'm on my way."

Relief. It pummels through my system. I need him here to help with Seth.

"Figured it wasn't her, just had to be sure. Have this gut feeling it's someone I least expect."

Revenge burns hot in the pit of my soul. Never in a million years did I think owning a sex club would come to this. Makes me want to toss in the towel and give it all away.

"You need to listen to me, Logan. I watched you go

through hell after what Shadow did to Ellie. You come clean, or you'll never get to see the good side of life. Now, do you want me to find a way to pump Whitney full of lead before I fly home or do you want the honor?"

With the last word drilling a hole in my head, I reach my destination. Guilt and a whole heap of conflicted emotions are churning in my gut like acid.

Unhooking my phone from Bluetooth, I place it up to my ear as I park outside Ellie's store and take a look around. The black and white Ebony & Ivory sign dangles under a striped awning of the same colors, the pink and white one sprawled across the entire front of a cupcake shop next door, a bright yellow neon awning for the coffee shop across the street, a blue one for the book store a few doors down. Her little corner of the world is colorful and lively. So much like her, I can't help but feel a sense of pride. Like I had the right to be proud of how far Ellie has come as I take in her family store.

I'll be damned if I let some jealous, stark raving bitch come along and upturn Ellie's life.

Bitterness rips at my lungs. A denial I want to believe that if Ellie knew the secret I was keeping, she'd forgive me.

"No. Shadow is the one I want. Whitney is yours or Rocco's. Just get her back on the streets. I want her crawling to me before she dies. Glad to have you coming home, Gabe. We all missed you, especially Lexi."

I can hear the smile on his face. He loves that girl more than anything. Pretty sure he's going to trip all over Ellie too.

"And, Seth?" Worry trips through the line.

"Needs help." I've never seen Seth quite like this. He's spiraling and fuck all if he listens.

Frustrated as hell, I hang up, climb out of my car, hit the locks and with every step I take, my deceit suffocates me a little more, the walls inching closer in on me. Won't be long until I am no longer able to breathe.

Pushing open the door, I take a good look around the place. In one corner of the large room are two brightly colored overstuffed chairs, a vibrant pink couch, shelves lined with throw pillows on distressed wood shelving. Jewels in glassed-in showcases, clothes neatly hanging on the back wall.

The place is an organized mess.

Chaos, unlike me who likes everything neatly in place.

The look of this place doesn't surprise me a bit. Goes to show how opposites attract.

Making my way a little farther into the room, instead of seeing the woman I'm dying to set my eyes on, I'm met by a woman with dreadlocks down to her waist, hipster style clothing, and a dirty look that would knock most men on their ass.

Lucky for me, I'm not most men.

Ellie told me to prepare myself for the wrath that might unfold. Not sure I'm ready because the woman's glare should knock me dead. I get the feeling she's a lot like Ellie, not afraid to bite her tongue. Makes me respect her more than I already do. Any person who takes someone and raises them as their own are people I regard highly.

"I'm Logan Mitchell; you must be Renita?"

I take the box she's holding from her hands, place it on the counter and stand there waiting for the glaring woman to give me a piece of her mind.

"I am. I'm going to warn you once. Don't hurt my girl. If you even think about bringing filth anywhere near her, I will make life hell for you. You might be new, but you tell her goodbye before you cheat. And God, the Devil, your people, not one of them will save you from me. I will die for Ellie. I will kill for Ellie. I expect you to get rid of Shadow, do you hear? My Ellie is a good person. She will give all she has. If I find out you pulled the wool over her eyes in any way, I don't care how much money you have; I will ruin you in ways money can't buy. If you're any kind of man, you'll stay true to your word. If you don't, then you are just like Shadow. Now give me your hand so I can shake it properly."

My chest tightens. I feel her warning. I feel it everywhere inside of me, punching my lungs, stabbing my mind, tossing in my stomach.

I honestly don't think the repercussions, the possibility of the damage I could do to Ellie assaults me until right this minute, standing less than a foot in front of a woman about as tiny as a fairy giving me her threatening motherly advice.

Little does she know, hurting Ellie is the last thing I want to do. The problem is, I'm not quite sure how to stop it.

"I don't plan on it."

Damn lie.

Fuck, how I wish the holy waters could cleanse them away. If it did, I wouldn't be hurting Ellie at all because she wouldn't have gone through what she did if I would have manned-up and introduced myself years ago.

I swallow that shit down, demanding for the time being to purge what happened to Ellie out of my mind.

"You better make sure it stays that way."

I doubt it, lady. Doubt Ellie will want a damn thing to do with me when I break her.

And I will.

I give her my hand as she asked. Have half a notion of bending down and kissing it. Letting her know how happy I am Ellie has her in her corner.

"Hey, did the two of you meet? You weren't too hard on him, were you?" Ellie's voice is sure and solid coming out of lips painted bright red as she closes a door I'm assuming leads to her apartment and stops next to Renita, their gazes never wavering from one another.

I've never seen such a wide assortment of emotions flash

UNRAVEL

over someone's features with such transparency as I do when Ellie reaches for Renita and hugs her. Pure adoration. It lights up both women's entire faces. I didn't think it was possible for Ellie to look anymore beautiful, but seemingly, I was wrong. She loves this woman — a mother and child bond.

No bloodlines needed.

Fuck me. I'm a dirty rotten prick.

"He's still standing, isn't he?"

"Renita," Ellie scolds, then busts out laughing. It's a beautiful sound even if it's directed at me.

Renita shrugs, pulling back and starts pulling clothes out of the box I just took from her.

I nearly stagger and drop to my knees when Ellie flashes her beautiful face toward me. She is nothing like the women I'm used to being with — the ones who give themselves to me in hopes of getting more than a good fuck.

Those sharp-like talons of theirs hoping to sink into my flesh, open up my coal colored heart as much as they try to pry open my wallet. I'd forgotten how good it felt to want something and not get it with a snap of my fingers.

And, goddamn do I ever want all of her sweetness and the vinegar she possesses.

Fuck, I need to feel her in my arms. Smell her honey scent and kiss the hell out of her. I hold back like I did when she was on the back of my bike a few nights ago, squeezing those legs around mine, her breasts rubbing against my back. I wanted to pull into some abandoned parking lot, strip her bare, release my cock and tell her to ride me.

The woman is painfully gorgeous to look at. Christ Almighty, I want to keep her.

"You look gorgeous." And she does standing there in a pair of jeans, cowgirl boots and a light blue silk top that has to be tied at the neck by the way it slants inward, clings to her breasts, and exposes her elegant neck.

Shit, it's going to be hard not to stare at all that exposed flesh around those tits, even harder to get my hands to obey, and not undo the back, letting the silk fall and bear those coin-sized nipples to my vision.

"It was nice to meet you, Logan. I'll lock up; have a good time, sweetheart. I'll be leaving for Rachelle's after this. You call me anytime." Renita says the last with a deadly glare in her eyes.

"Okay. Take care of your sister and tell her she's going to be fine."

Ellie had filled me in on Renita's impromptu trip to Nashville to help her older sister get around. The woman was in a car accident and broke a leg and an arm.

I'd offer help, but something tells me Renita wouldn't take it.

A memory betrays me with flashes of the way Ellie kissed me with those plump lips as she bends, kisses Renita and draws her in for another hug.

The way she wrapped those arms around me letting herself open up and gave me her body. *Me.* A man who doesn't deserve her.

The woman owns natural beauty, all the while carrying a riveting erotic side to her that she's unaware of. Ellie Wynn is an addiction no man would be able to cure.

And, I'm the goddamn asshole who's going to wilt her to nothing.

I stand here repeating to myself that tonight isn't about seduction; it's about getting to know one another more. Finding out the things I don't know about her, letting Ellie see another side of me I don't allow people to see.

"Ready?" she asks, staring up at me, those lips parting, and fuck me, this woman makes it damn easy to relax just by being in her space.

Awareness sparks between us, swear the smile lighting up Ellie's face is due to her seeing the bright embers fall to the floor. Kind of hard to miss.

Explosive.

Red-hot smoking flames burn brighter than they did yesterday when I rubbed her upper thigh while leaving the city behind. I had half a notion of disappearing.

"The question is, are you ready?" I challenge, watching the wonder of where we're going build across her brow.

We bid Renita goodbye, and I take hold of Ellie's hand, guiding her across the street and helping her into my Mercedes and lifting my chin at my detail as I round the back before climbing into the driver's seat.

"To answer your question, I'm ready for this date. Not quite sure if I'm ready for a man like you, Logan Mitchell. Are you worth the risk, worth the breaking of my heart to get to the core of yours?"

Jesus Christ, I wish I was worthy.

I clench my hands around the steering wheel, pulling onto the street before my idea of proving anything to her is overridden by the thoughts of her sitting on my face.

Her words hang in the air as we zip through the streets. I'm unsafe to the honesty this woman has. Know it so deep that responding to her would open that can holding one giant lie I'd never be able to set right. The fact I was willing to ruin this date and spill it at her feet shows just how much of an asshole I am.

"Where are we going?"

"My place, I promise my intentions are pure. Dinner and watching the sunset surrounded by the trees and you."

Up until Gabe called, my plans weren't wholesome; I intended on having her in some way. Mouth wrapped around my dick with my tongue buried in between her thighs was the first thing that came to mind. Now, I just want to talk to her.

"Really? That field and the view is my favorite part of your estate. My dad used to call me his bonnet. We used to have a field full of Texas bluebonnets. He died in an oil rig explosion. I lost my mother a few years earlier. I have a feeling you know this already."

Sadness drips from her voice. Of course, I know about her parents. More about her father's death than her mother's, the endearment part is a bit shocking. Although for me it's another unique quality about Ellie.

"Yes. There is plenty I don't know," I tell her, hoping to reassure any doubt.

My eyes move to those distracting plump lips. I've kissed as many women as I've fucked. Always part of the seduction. This woman though, I could devour her mouth and kiss her for hours without it leading anywhere. It seems ever since meeting Ellie, everything inside of me wants to change.

The ride to my place is made up of mostly talking on her part. I ask questions, and she answers. Her face lights up when she answers my question about her relationship with Renita and how they came about opening the store. The three of them thought it was ideal because they'd spent a lot of time shopping in consignment stores. How her and Norah's college business degrees would help, and with Renita's sense of style, it was the right decision and the best one they've made.

"Renita sounds like a good woman."

"She is. I don't know where I'd be today without her or Norah."

A spear of fury stabs me like a dull blade — the need to protect this woman all the more. The need to hunt and maim and mutilate whoever hired someone to hurt her is so strong

I have to talk myself down by the time we made it to my estate and stepped inside my home.

"You need to decorate, Logan," Ellie whispers from beside me. Her tone indicating an explanation as to why my house is empty.

"I know. I've owned this place for years and haven't done much except my bedroom and office. Feel free to share ideas." Truth. I have owned it for years. Lie. I rarely stay here. It was much more convenient to stay at the apartment above the club.

"Really? Something tells me my taste is quite different from yours."

"Try me." Needing to stop this conversation before shit gets too heavy. I take hold of Ellie's hand and head toward the kitchen, grab the picnic basket I packed up, and by the time we make it down the path of trees into the clearing the previous owner set up with a picnic table, fire pit, and chairs, I figure we have about a half hour before the sun sets.

Watching Ellie's reaction to the sun going down when she was here the night of my party was what captured my attention before it went in the gutter after seeing her standing in a sexy short dress. Those legs bare. I wanted to drop to my knees, lick them and spread them wide. And when she turned her back to avoid me, the blood drained from my face to my dick. All I wanted was to run the tip of my finger down her spine and grab hold of her tight ass.

"I can see why your father called you Bonnet. Your eyes are the same color. I've never seen a woman as beautiful as you." Those words are some of the most honest ones I've spoken.

"Thank you." A blush hits her neck and rises to her cheeks, a timid smile spreads across those full lips.

Taking in a much-needed lungful of air, I inhale her light scent. She smells like freshness, like our surroundings.

Intoxicating.

There's more to Ellie than beauty. She's brave and fascinating, and that sexual side of her is begging to come out.

I have this feeling once it does, we'll both discover a pleasure neither of us knew existed.

"Wow, this looks great. Simple and romantic. Who knew Logan Mitchell had a bit of romance in him," she whispers, tossing her head back, easy laughter spilling out of her mouth after she pulls out a bowl of fruit, and individual peanut butter and jelly sandwiches, single bags of chips and a bottle of wine. I want to laugh right with her, but when she slings one long leg over the bench of the table, I stop her from sitting down, hook her around the waist, and follow by throwing a leg of my own over and tugging her onto my lap.

The agony is real. I need to touch her.

Tangling my fingers in her hair, I guide her head downward, slant my mouth over hers, and I take. Soft, warm lips surrender and open, and I plunge my hungry tongue into her mouth.

Pants break free from the back of her throat, fingers clinging to my shoulders. I fist a hand in her hair and yank.

Ellie stares at me, examining my face, looking at me like she is curious and afraid out of her mind. Like she wants to explore and ask and give and take. Like she was wondering who the hell this man is that has been coming on strong, and now he's half gentleman, half beast. Like she is silently begging to fix whatever hides underneath me.

If only I knew how to let her. Regard her reaction before I soil and contaminate.

Fucking Christ.

It won't be long before I'm drowning the both of us in murky quicksand with no one to lend a hand to pull us out.

Shit.

My dick twitches when she begins to shift her ass over him — grinding for a little relief.

It feels right, but damn it all to hell is it wrong.

Slowly, I take my time exploring that neck. Her back arches ever so slightly, welcoming to nip and tease. The animal in me wants to mark it with a bite. I settle for running my nose up the side, the feel of her shivering on my lap, my hips slowly thrusting upward, hers grinding down is making me painfully hard.

A gasp falls from her mouth, lips shockingly parted. She feels so good in my arms, trembles wracking through her, nipples hard as she presses her tight little body into my chest.

"Logan."

"Needed a taste, the next move is up to you, Ellie."

Bright blue-violet eyes take in my face. Mainly my mouth. As if the beauty wasn't sure she heard what I said.

"You get off on driving me crazy, don't you?"

I feel my life of debauchery covering my eyes as I assess how to answer her question. "I do, Ellie. Foreplay is sweet torture. It'll make fucking you again better than it was the first time around."

"It better." She sighs, stopping her movements with a little frustrated moan. Swear to God, that sexy sound could kill a man where he stands.

I want to take back my words and fuck her until she screams for mercy.

Adjusting her next to me, I change the subject. I tell her a story I've never told anyone before — a time in my life when things weren't so fucked up and blurred.

"These sandwiches are made with my mother's homemade recipe. Strawberries, blackberries, and blueberries. My older brother, Lane, and his daughter, Lexi, made the jelly. I have a younger brother, Seth, too, the three of us used to help our mom make it, then after we lost our dad in a car accident, she got lost, ended up killing herself. But Lane, he kept on trying to make the jelly until one day it turned out right. I don't know, a fond memory of when things were perfect. What about you, what's one of your favorite childhood memories?"

"I'm sorry about your parents."

I shrug. "They're gone. Nothing I can do about it. My father, Liam, I miss him. The bitch who born me, not so much. After they died, we were taken in by family friends. Kind of like you." We sit and eat while I fill her in on Gabe and Lena. Ellie doesn't bat an eye when I let her in on Gabe being mafia. "Now we have Lexi, my niece. She's Lane's."

Ellie's blue gaze bounces to mine.

"I'd love to meet her sometime."

"I'd like that too." And Christ I would, Lexi probably more.

"I was seven, and my father took my mother and me out on one of his offshore oil rigs, he used to take us all the time. He named it The Wynn; it was his first one. We sat on the helicopter pad and watched the sunset, tossing flower petals into the water, and my mom looked at my father and said this is my favorite place. As awful as this might sound, my father died on that rig. Besides being with Mom and me, it was his favorite place to be too, not because he owned it, because of the view."

I gulp around the ball of fire blazing in my throat.

A tremble crawls down my spine. Fingers are reaching inside and squeezing tight. Faces, so many endless women's faces, and non-meaningful nights I wasted when all along I could have spent them listening to her.

I've done some messed up shit in my life, but one thing I've never done is given up. Once she knows everything about me, I won't let Ellie walk away without a fight.

She is priceless.

CHAPTER 15

Ellie

"Hello?" I call into the lifeless house, pushing open the door and closing it softly.

"There's a doorbell, you know."

I look up at where Maggie, Logan's secretary, stands at the bottom of the stairs. Hands on her hips. Her boobs practically spilling out of her too small bikini top.

"Excuse me, let me step out and ring the bell so the lady of the house can let me in." I roll my eyes.

I don't like her. The overconfident way she lifts her brows as if she wishes I would do just that makes me want to knock her off her high-heels. Who the hell wears heels with a bathing suit? Other than beauty contestants, and this one isn't a queen at all. She's a jealous tramp like the rest.

"Don't bother, I'll let Logan know you're here to see him." She tilts her head to the side, studies me briefly before starting to walk away.

"Maggie, Logan invited me, you know very well why I'm here and it isn't for a business meeting. I'm very capable of letting the guy I'm dating know myself. Piece of advice, wipe the jealousy off your face, it doesn't fit you any better than that godawful swimsuit does." I allow my eyes to roam up and down her body. As childish as my words are, she isn't going to treat me like garbage.

When she turns on a little huff, her heels clicking on the floor, I smile in spite of stooping to her level.

Driving here, I had no idea what I was about to find, but when I pulled up and saw guards at the gates, I had a feeling they were in plain sight for me, and not hiding as Logan told me they usually are.

I'm sure they have everything to do with Logan still searching for who hurt me. It could have been Maggie, for all I know. I'd think Logan would trust her though.

I sure don't.

He warned me there was going to be women here and not to trust a single one. As if I would anyway.

I could be heading for a disaster. Quite honestly, I shouldn't care. I'm not here for those people, and if any of them try to intimidate me like Maggie tried, they'll get a hushed, harsh lashing from my tongue.

I pause, all thoughts of anyone else flying out the door I just came through. My face heats up when I spot the floor to ceiling windows. I have a feeling those are the windows where Logan's big body brought my spirit to soar.

The crazy thing is, I'd never cared that a touch, a kiss, a man was missing from my life. Not until Logan Mitchell bulldozed right through my solid walls. I wasn't prepared for how his touch makes me feel. How I crave more of it; how his hands are capable of worshipping me just by holding mine.

Logan makes me realize how lost I was and how happy I am he's the one who found me.

It's unbelievable, and now I'm about to meet the only other female in his life — the one person whose first impression of me matters the most. Plus, his brothers'. I owe Seth more than I can ever repay him for. And, Lane. I'm just all around anxious to meet him.

This past week with Logan has been magical, also a lot confusing. All we've done is ask and answer questions about one another. At times he seemed lost. Giving me a strong sense he has something else he wants to unload off his chest.

Logan is making me need things I'd never thought I'd need. Things I had a pretty good sense of judgment would make me fall too quickly if I gave in as I did before. I'm positive he sensed it too, and that's why he told me the next move was mine, so instead of pressuring me, all the big man has done is kiss me, and I'm ready for more.

Aching and splintering into pieces.

Hiking my bag over my shoulder, I gaze around the spacious foyer, letting my mind take everything in until my eyes become dazed when I observe what's sitting in the living room.

A surprised gasp escapes my lungs. I smile so wide my face hurts.

I'm stunned.

Knocked with excitement so boundless it nearly drops me to my knees.

"He bought the furniture I showed him."

At first, when Logan said he wanted ideas, I was shocked. It didn't take a day until my excitement got the best of me, and I was searching online like a girl gone mad. When I ran across these pieces, I knew they were Logan. And he just up and bought them.

Unbelievable.

Brown rustic worn leather furniture surrounded by light wood tables and a bold abstract colorful area rug rest around the river rock fireplace with a large flat screen television above the mantel. This design is full of texture and depth. It's a class of its own.

It's perfect. Homey and I love it.

"You surprise me at every turn on this long drive. There's still a lot of roads left to cover, a lot to know about you, Logan Mitchell," I whisper. I know I won't like some of it, but as long as it stays in his past, it won't make me like him less.

Trust.

It's bending his way a little more.

I straighten myself out and start making my way toward the kitchen. I'm going to make sure today is a great day despite whoever is here.

Logan brought up a birthday party for his niece he was hosting today, asking me if I wanted to come. I said yes, and when I asked him to tell me about Lexi and the things she liked, our eyes locked, mine curious to know everything as well as thankful he wanted me to meet his family. And his lighting up in shock, it was almost as if he was stunned someone would care enough to want to know them. As if no one ever sincerely asked before.

I found myself sinking in the depths of his dark, dark ocean colored orbs as he talked fondly about Lexi and his brothers. Even though I listened to every word he said, I couldn't help letting my mind wander. I swear the man reminds me of a cliffhanger at the end of a book, one you never saw coming yet stays on your brain, one you want to study the pages, frightened, yet intrigued, and so damn anxious to get to the next book. To figure what's happening with the big secret that left you hanging at the end.

Logan's a thriller. One big giant man full of secrets and I've willingly hopped in the driver seat. All I can do from here is pray we don't crash and burn.

"Logan, I'm here?"

Laughter in the form of little girl giggles drags me

through the still empty dining room. I pause when I enter the luxurious kitchen that I fell in love with before. There's a nook with a large bay window looking over the magnolia trees. The view would be one I'd admire every day. It doesn't hold my attention as much as the room that looks like no one has ever used.

"What a shame."

Everything is white. Not a splash of color in sight, unless you'd call the stainless steel appliances a color. Not a coffee pot on the counter, no fruit on the small long island in the middle of the room.

This home needs brought to life.

"This is a far cry from the lively colorful exterior. If I didn't know better, I'd swear Logan moved out."

I jump, letting out a squeal when a shirtless man strides through the door. Big and tall and wide.

"Shit, I'm sorry." His voice rough.

"It's okay. I'm Ellie; Logan invited me."

I raise my head to get a better look at the man, and my eyes bug out. My mouth is drying up instantly. Good Lord, the sight of this man has me placing my hand on my chest. He looks so much like Logan it's scary.

Droplets of water drip down his face from his long jet-black hair, and when he runs his fingers through it, twisting it into a ponytail, those eyes as green as Logan's probe deep with a divided sadness as he takes me in.

Nervously, I approach him, a little ruffled and wondering which one of his brothers he is. Whatever one, he has some horrible demons living inside of him.

"I'm Seth, and this trouble maker here is the birthday girl, Lexi Mae. We were coming in to get her Ariel cake. Weren't we, little mermaid?"

His words are slurred, jagged and worn around the edges as are his tired eyes. I dare to think he's halfway to being drunk. The one thing Logan told me he was hoping Seth wouldn't be.

But I'm glad to meet him and give him the thanks he deserves finally.

Collecting myself, I take a few steps toward him and look down to where the little girl stands grasping onto her uncle's leg. Blonde hair in two long braids aside her cute little face, so pretty with big blue eyes staring up at me in curiosity. I fall in love with her instantly.

I turn toward Seth and nearly stop breathing when he breaks into a smile, eyes swirling with intensity and alcohol I'd be able to smell a mile away as he takes hold of my hand and brings it to his lips.

A gentleman with secrets. Just like his brother.

"Nice to meet you. Thank you for what you did for me, Seth. I might not be standing here if it wasn't for you."

He cringes as if my words slice right through him.

I'd dare to think this grown man has rarely heard a sincere thank you in his life.

God, what the hell happened to the Mitchell brothers? It's almost like they miss having a woman in their lives who genuinely care.

It's one of the saddest thoughts ever to cross my mind.

"I'm sorry I didn't get there before he hurt you. I promised Logan nothing would happen to you. I let him and you down. It seems my promises are going to shit," he whispers, blame and shame and self-loathing not hard to pick up from his gruff voice.

"It's not your fault. Let's not bring it up again."

He wavers for a second as if he can't believe I'd accept his apology, before he nods, let's go of my hand and looks off to something behind me.

It's unnerving, those piercing eyes of his despite the

sincerity in them is holding something else inside. Something I'm all too quick to understand.

Pain and grief.

I'm drawn with a need so fierce to hug the man. To tell him he isn't as bad as he might think he is.

Seth's look reminds me of one I've caught on Logan many times. This particular gaze is one of the things I've come to learn about Logan. He thinks he isn't worthy of me. I can see it every time he takes me in.

Makes me wonder if Lane holds something inside of him too.

"You said a bad word, Uncle Sef. The S-word is fifty cents in the swear word jar."

I can't help it; I let out a laugh.

"You better forgive me or no present for you, little girl." He tugs on her braids causing Lexi to giggle and shake her head.

"No way. Today is my day. You haf to pay up, or I'm telling Daddy."

Adorable is the word that comes to mind when I hear her speak. She can't yet grasp onto her Ts. I bend down to become eye level with Lexi, and as I do, Seth shakes his head and walks past me without another word.

"Happy birthday, Lexi. Your hair sure is pretty."

She smiles, dimples and all.

"I like yours too; it looks just like mine."

Logan informed me how much Lexi loves to swim. Not having any idea if I'd get into the pool, I decided to braid my hair.

"Guess that makes us twins then."

"Yup and my name is special too. Lexi, it means I'm super smart and pretty. But Daddy calls me his princess."

There went my heart. "Want to know how else were alike?"

"Yes." She squeals, her little eyes going wide.

"My middle name is Mae. The same as yours."

"No way. Wait until I tell my daddy. We're really twins. Except you're a queen and I'm a princess."

God, this little thing is precious. Even I can see it, and I'm not around children very often. It was clear when Logan spoke about her, she's the most treasured person in his life. I can see why. Lexi is the light to his dark.

She's these men's entire world, and if that isn't proof they aren't bad, then I don't know what will.

Makes me wonder if he sees me the same way.

Logan keeps revealing a little more of his good every time I see him, digging himself just a little deeper.

I cannot deny any longer I'm drawn in a way I might never understand.

A strong pull.

He needed me in his life as much as I needed him.

With a smile, I lift my head, then freeze when my vision rolls over the giant of a man standing in the doorway. My breath catches in my throat, blood pounding hard in my ears. He has to be Lane, and he's also the biggest of the three. Damn, it's no wonder women fall all over these men. They are strikingly handsome with those deep bad boy vibes that draw you in.

"That's right; you are a princess and my favorite girl. Thank you for coming today, Ellie. Lexi has been waiting to meet you. We all have. I'm Lane." I take his hand and melt a little when he kisses my knuckles. "The guests are waiting for you, princess; we need the cake and then it's time for presents."

Lane is wearing swim shorts too. His skin free of ink, all except a red rose across his heart dripping with teardrop shapes of blood. He's just as dangerous and intoxicating as his brothers. He has the same eyes with a lot less coldness.

But there's something dark and threatening about him — a bit of rigidity and a whole lot of heartache.

"My pleasure, Lane. I wouldn't have missed this for the world." I shake his offered hand. There's warmth and kindness behind it; even so, I can see he holds the same kind of sadness as his brothers.

These brothers are a riddle. A complex one I don't dare try to solve. Not when I haven't fully unraveled their older brother.

Neglect and abuse. It's clear as day that's the foundation to the three of them — a wide range of grief and heartache and pain.

"Okay, Daddy. I need to tell my new best friend something first, okay?" Lexi wraps her arms around Lane's legs, her voice loud and confident.

"It's your day, baby. Just don't talk her head off."

I snag a lift of his brows before I shift my gaze back to Lexi and give her my attention.

"Daddy, Ellie's head can't come off from me talking. Geez. I'm five now, Ellie. Uncle Logan said he'd buy me a new Ariel doll if I were good, I've been super good. The bestest I can be. I don't need a new doll, 'cause I sleep with the one Uncle Sef bought me, but I wanted an Ariel cake, so Uncle Logan bought me one. He doesn't know how to cook. My daddy does. He makes the best mac and cheese and grits. Do you like grits?" She pauses, scrunches up her nose as she looks up at her father once again, more than likely silently gathering the courage to finish what she wants to say. "I have monies in my backpack. Do you like Ariel, 'cause, 'cause, she's playing at the movies and Daddy has taken me twice. I want to see her again."

Her cuteness wrenches in my chest.

"The movies? If it's okay with your daddy, I'll go with

you. I used to watch it with my dad when I was a little girl. Grits and Ariel are my favorite."

Tears, they sting my eyes when I think about the gift I brought. A little mermaid costume that my mother made for me. I dragged it out of storage yesterday, washed and ironed it. The thing looks brand new. It's one of the few things I have left of my mother. And, I have it because Renita snatched it along with several other costumes when she was fired.

"Can she, Daddy?"

Lane clears his throat. "Of course she can take you, sweetie. Excuse me; I have no idea where Seth went. Lexi, please take Ellie out to Uncle Logan. Thank you again, Ellie."

Gratitude passes through his eyes, and I'm not sure why I sense he wants to say more, maybe about the absence of his daughter's mother. I don't know where she is; I do know Logan told me she hasn't been in their lives since the day she had her. Makes me admire Lane all the more. The guy is mother and father to his daughter. It's just as much endearing as sad.

"You're welcome, Lane." Purpose settles inside me right then and there. No matter what happens between Logan and me, I'll find a way to remain in this little girl's life.

Rejecting the heavy lump that wants to lodge itself deep in my stomach, I force myself up and grip hold of the bag containing Lexi's gift. When Logan mentioned how obsessed she is with Disney princesses, mostly, The Little Mermaid, I knew right away the costume would be perfect for her and my mother would want her to have it.

I can still feel my fingers tracing the soft material on the fins. Remembering my dad bending down and tying them around my ankles. The look of adoration as he adjusted the bright green skirt with a tulle overlay.

The way he took hold of my hand and we'd people watch,

well, he would, I mostly asked questions as we walked the streets collecting candy on Halloween while Mom stayed home to hand some out.

I remember my father explaining that just because we all look, dress, or act differently, it doesn't mean people aren't kind. He taught me to give and not expect anything in return. He taught me many things. However, as I grew to understand how life worked, I've done everything in me to live by one thing he showed me more than anything else. To be kind to those who deserve it, because there are very few things in this world that don't come with a price. And kindness is one of them.

But when I step outside, and Lexi points to where Logan is standing with a group of women before she takes off running toward a half dozen or so little girls. A familiar twinge runs up my arms, and it isn't kindness. It's filled with dread — a strong sense of hatred.

Someone here wants to do more than hurt me.

They want me dead.

CHAPTER 16

Logan

"I like your friend, Uncle Logan. She's pretty, has the same middle name as me and likes The Little Mermaid and, and she has the same color hair as Snow White. That means she's not a queen like you said, Ellie is a princess like me."

Lexi throws me a sweet glance, her little finger resting at the corner of her mouth, nose scrunched like it always is when she's thinking. At the moment, it's as if her brain is adding up all the reasons why she likes Ellie.

I fling my gaze from the cuteness toward the woman she's rattling on about, Ellie has my girl wrapped as much as me. Standing over there so sincere and fascinating as she talks with Lane and Gabe, all that black hair weaved in two sexy as fuck braids.

I want to tug on them like reins while I ram into her from behind.

It's hotter than hell out here, and she has me sweating more than this unbearable heat. So beautiful and noticeable, it's hard to ignore her.

Blinding. Just like the sun.

My conscience starts bashing against my skull, a reminder that I'm a disgusting piece of shit.

"You do, huh? I like her too."

And that's the thing; I do like her — a hell of a lot.

My heart skids to a stop in my chest when Lexi grips my face, pushing my cheeks together and leaning in until our noses touch, face all serious, eyes big and round like her mother.

Damn good thing her worthless mom isn't around or this precious girl wouldn't be who she is — all sweet and pure.

"Don't tell Daddy this. I heard him tell Uncle Sef you were going to hurt Ellie. Hurting people is bad, Uncle Logan. Ellie is my friend now so you can't hurt her, or I'll be mad at you forever and ever."

My lungs draw in air. Didn't think the pressure in my chest could weigh me down any further.

It does, from words of a little girl who just put me in my place.

"I won't hurt her, sweetheart."

Another reason why I'm going to Hell slips out of my mouth — lying to a five-year-old. My insides vibrate with my death sentence, and my black heart jumps into my throat.

Heavy and hurting and dripping with poison.

"Okay. Thanks for the party, Uncle Logan, and my gift. Ellie said she'd teach me how to make the friendship bracelets you gave me."

Jesus Christ.

Ellie's sincere kindness is dripping off her worse than my sweat.

Decent and wholesome. Humble and genuine. All kinds of right and I don't deserve forgiveness because I'm unquestionably a dark storm creeping in to destroy her light. To shut it off and swallow the beauty and goodness in my pool of deceit and unforgivable betrayal.

Still doesn't stop me from wanting between her legs. To give her more pleasure than I did before. Watch her beg and shake and come hard around my cock.

I choke down my lie, those emotions kicking in as Lexi takes off running, her swimsuit hidden underneath the Little Mermaid costume Ellie gave her. One I have a feeling was hard for Ellie to part with.

The woman is a saint with all kinds of steamy desire begging to get out. I need inside her soon, or I'm going to explode.

Lust has been hanging in the air. It started when Ellie sat and played with Lexi and her little friends — only making me want her more.

And even though I wanted to march her perky ass anywhere but out here where she's been looked at as if she was intruding, I knew if I did, we'd be spending the rest of the day with her tied up in bed — fucking like wild animals.

I rise, finish my beer and remove the rest of the leftover hot dogs off the grill. The second I turn to take them into the house, Lauren — a woman I used to fuck on the regular, and who I've pretty much ignored all her little taunts and teases of sexual fantasies she's whispered in my ear all day —meets me at the slider and takes the plate from my hand and carries it into my kitchen.

Bitches are all standing around in the air-conditioned house. They moved inside less than five minutes after Ellie arrived watching her through the goddamn window.

They shouldn't be in the kitchen if they can't take the heat from a beautiful woman that puts them to shame.

Worthless, and here I tapped into shit like that.

Fuck.

Makes me wonder if any of them are the ones who went after her. Whoever did is like a ghost.

I take a seat to watch Ellie part from Lane and Gabe and wander around with Lexi and her friends. My cock jerking as she bends down to the girl's eye level and I catch a glimpse of what I'm sure are bottoms to a pink bikini.

Sensual as any one woman could be. The kind of woman that if a man had a chance, he wouldn't want to fall asleep at night out of fear he'd wake, and she wouldn't be real.

That taste I had was nothing compared to what this woman can give me. Knew the minute I buried myself inside her it didn't matter how many times I saw her, how many times I tasted her, it was never going to be enough.

Ellie is sweet and sinful. Brave and beautiful, a fiery blaze of a million bright stars twinkling in the night. Sexy and seductive.

My cock stirs, and my chest tightens. Emotions that fuck with my head, coming out of nowhere.

Decency.

Morals.

Ethics.

They are all I hear, all I've been thinking about since I kissed her the first time.

Momentarily, what grabs my attention is the way Ellie picks up handfuls of magnolia petals, rubs her fingers across the silky flower before dropping to her knees and placing handfuls into each girl's cupped hands.

That woman symbolizes the description of sexy in a way I've never noticed in a woman before. She is the entire package of everything any man would want to wrap up and claim as their own. She's down to earth, doesn't give a shit if she gets dirty and she's the only woman here who has given her undivided attention to the kids.

Also, Ellie is the only person who brought a gift that was

worth more to Lexi than any other she received. Everyone else brought clothes and expensive jewelry. I mean for fuck's sake, who the hell gives a five-year-old a gold bracelet? The rich assholes I hang out with, that's who.

Fuck me straight to hell.

"Here you go, Logan; you look like you could use another." Lauren sets a beer on the table next to me. Her tits hard to ignore, spilling out of her too tight bikini top as she leans over a little longer than necessary.

Lauren is beautiful, and she's the kind of woman I could easily slip away with and fuck. The type of woman reminding me who I was, and what I enjoyed doing. She studies me, her eyes shooting down to my cock. I try imagining my dick sliding between the crack of her ass right before I lube her up with juices dripping out of her and fuck her tight little behind, making her scream. The image disgusts me. My dick doesn't even twitch, but my mind does in loathing at the thought.

"Thanks. Don't know what game you think you're playing. You and everyone else know I'm off limits. Not going back, Lauren. Stay away from Ellie and me or suffer consequences that'll hurt your daughter. Make sure you spread the word to your fake friends inside *my* house. I'm done with it all, you understand?" I leave the beer where she placed it as she huffs and walks away without another word. Bitch knows when enough is enough.

I'm no longer thirsty anyway when I'd much rather get a buzz from the woman who has taken my niece under her wing.

"Jesus, I think my daughter is infatuated with Ellie as much as you are." Lane plops down in the seat next to me and crosses his feet at the ankles. Gabe takes the bottle of beer, tosses it in the trash and sits in the other. My heart rate kicks up, a punch of unease hitting my senses.

I'm about to get ambushed.

"That she does. Ellie's good, Lane. Don't pull your protection shit and not let her spend time with Lexi because of me." Watching Ellie give her undivided attention to Lexi is what my niece needs. A woman who cares.

"Fuck you. That woman right there is what my kid needs — someone who isn't going to screw her over. I hope you're considering telling Ellie soon. You're out of your comfort zone, asshole, and if you don't choose your next move wisely, you'll be doing more damage than you can fix."

"What the hell is that supposed to mean?" I know what he's going on about without him having to clarify. Regardless, he isn't going to guilt trip me by tossing Lexi in my face no matter how much he's right.

"Fate, brother, she's a wise bitch. My daughter's mother didn't give a fuck she was given the best gift a person could get. Our mother didn't either. Take a hard look at Ellie with those girls. They are sitting in the dirt, putting flowers in each other's hair and making bracelets. I have to believe Ellie's in our lives for more than her being a plaything for you. I'm referring to you doing what's right no matter what, Logan. Ellie doesn't want you for your money; she's long term. She's a one-man woman. Quit thinking with your dick for once in your life."

I run a thumb over my bottom lip, contemplating my answer, when what I'd love to do is plow my fist into his truthful mouth.

"I know what kind of woman Ellie is. You don't need to remind me."

"Yeah, right. I'm beginning to wonder if you do. Not one of these bitches would drop in the dirt, let alone say yes when a kid asks to go to the movies. Hell, they don't even take their own. Bet you didn't know she told Lexi she'd take her? Woman doesn't even know my daughter and she's over there making her see how special she is. Ellie deserves better, my daughter deserves to have a woman figure in her life, and I might love you, man, but my little girl, she comes before your game."

"It's not a game." Fuck him, he knows it's not.

"The two of you keep your goddamn voices down before you give the crazies more shit to go on about. Listen to the two of you fighting with each other when you got the same blood running through your veins. Support each other, stand by each other and help figure out a solution."

"There's only one solution, Gabe. You know it as well as I do. It's called the truth." My brother's words simmer with anger.

"For fuck's sake, Lane, walk in Logan's shoes and ask yourself what you would have done."

I bow my head, Gabe's tone hemorrhaging with sympathy. I don't want it. Don't deserve it.

A surge of guilt pulses at my veins as I watch Gabe head into the house, and a boulder lodges itself in my throat.

Silence falls upon Lane and me. The wedge between growing wide.

"I want more with her. I'm running out of time, Lane. I can feel it. I care about her. Honest to God, I do. I don't know how to tell her, brother." The words fall from my mouth effortlessly. It's the first time I've admitted something I never thought I'd say.

"I know, Logan. I'm trying to save Ellie and you from being hurt. Tell her and then prove you're a changed man before it's too late. The longer you wait, the harder the fall."

My mind spins, and my heart pummels against the cage containing it. Hate, I could taste the bile of it crawling up my throat.

I lean forward, watching Ellie and Lexi. Their innocent

laughter is ringing through the dusk settling air as Ellie ties a bracelet around her tiny wrist, and Lexi smiles.

Ellie must feel the heaviness of my stare because her head jerks up, nose and cheeks looking a little sunburned, and I swear on my father's grave, the world sucks me into oblivion from the smile that spreads across her unforgettable face.

I rub a restless hand over my chin, mind battling my body with what to do.

"I love you, Logan. I'm not saying another word, that look in your eyes tells me all I need to know. Don't come running when she's gone."

I respect my brother who can barely stand the sight of me. I might not like the way he's lashing out his concern, but he's right, I've done made up my mind. I'm not telling her today. If I could get away with holding my secret forever, I would. I should have told her from the beginning. She might have forgiven me then.

My body stiffens as Lane walks away and Ellie glides like an angel toward me.

The second she's within reach, I stand, my hand firing out, and I grip her by the waist.

A gasp flies from her mouth, her hands sliding up my stomach and clinging to my shoulders.

Desperation. It's adhering to me like a new layer of skin.

"She's the cutest thing I've ever met. I was nervous about meeting her and your brothers and Gabe. Where did Seth disappear to?"

Probably passed out drunk somewhere in between two women.

"Not sure. Come here."

I take hold of her hand and walk us to the door leading into the pool house and press her against it the second I close it behind us.

Bringing her in here while Lexi's party is going on will likely cause another confrontation with Lane. I don't care.

"Once everyone leaves, I'm going to make sure you can think of nothing but me and have you begging for my mercy. I won't stop."

I focus on the way her lids grow heavy. I listen to her light breaths, sinking in the flawless depths of her gorgeousness. Her warmth and open heart, her body pressed against mine is a need I can't ignore.

I'll feel this woman inside me for a lifetime. For the first time in my life, I feel frantic and weak and defenseless.

And I have the proof of my weakness in my arms, her tight, hot cunt pressing into my thigh.

I can feel it now — that heavy feeling of never seeing Ellie again. Of wishing I could have peace in my life with a woman who would care about me for me.

Ellie calms me, and I've never had that feeling in my life.

My heart pounds when she slides her hand out of mine, palms my cock through my swim shorts and lets out one of those sexy as fuck moans.

Curling a hand at the nape of her neck, the other sliding up her thigh, I forget there are people outside. Couldn't care less for giving the women who see Ellie as a thorn in their side another reason to hate her, and tilt her head to the side so I can take hold of those lips I want to be wrapped around my cock.

The rise and fall of her chest speed up as I kiss the hell out of her and slip my hand underneath her bikini bottoms, sliding a finger through her slick wet heat.

"I want you moaning while I finger-fuck you to orgasm against the door, but if you scream, I'll stop."

Not giving her a chance to reply, I plunge my middle finger into her pussy, and nuzzle my face into her neck, her pulse fluttering like butterfly wings.

UNRAVEL

Rapid and frenzied.

"I can't wait to get you naked, legs spread wide, body shaking, pussy drenched, and mind on the edge, mouth begging me to slam inside and fuck you unconscious. That proof you wanted about me being clean. It's upstairs on my bed waiting for you." I blow out every word as I brush kisses down her neck.

Jesus, I'm so hard it hurts, balls aching and pulling tight.

"Take your hand off my cock and place them palm down on the door."

She lets out a strangled gasp, squeezes my bulge and obeys.

"Good girl."

Hell, why can't life be simple so she could always be mine?

I pump in and out, add another digit and revel in the way her muscles constrict around my fingers.

"God, what are you doing to me?" Unmistakable need laces through her tone.

"I don't know, Ellie. Whatever this is between us, I don't want to stop." A pang of remorse rushes through me causing my chest to rumble.

"I came all over my stomach last night wishing my seed was coating your walls. I yelled your name. I imagined you on your knees with my cock down your throat, my hands gripping hold of your head until I shot off inside. Spend the night with me, Ellie?"

"God, Logan. Yes, I'll stay." She pants and drops her head against the back of the door. I slant my mouth over hers; she's so close to coming undone. I need to taste her release as it slips from her tongue.

I ruthlessly drive my fingers in and out of her drenched desire, my cock like granite as I feel her start to fall apart. I want to worship every inch of her, taste her. Her channel is so warm, so fucking perfect I'm going to be straining the rest of the day. Fuck, she is so damn gorgeous. More when she's vulnerable and at my command like this.

"You need my cock as badly as I need to be inside you." My teeth nip at her earlobe. "So receptive to my touch. Fuck my fingers and take what you need. What only I can give you. I can't get enough. Can't wait to be inside you bare."

I've never been before. There were times I was tempted, times women begged, but I never did. Condoms are mandatory in our club anyway. Even the married couples are forced to use them.

I brush my thumb over her clit, and just like that, she shatters. Tremors are shaking her tight little body. Her pleasure is dripping into my hand.

She twists her fingers in my hair, yanking hard. Fuck, I love it when she goes wild on me.

She rides my hand, pumping those hips, tiny moans tripping out of her mouth while all the wicked things I want to do to her will soon slip through my fingers like sand.

Her body shakes, and she thrusts her hips forward, arches her back, and comes.

I unwillingly pull my fingers out of her, place them on her bottom lip and grow impossibly hard as she sucks me clean. All I can picture is my cock sunk between those lips, but I need to get us back out there before shit hits the fan.

"Thank you for what you did for Lexi. For everything you're doing for her." Probably isn't the best timing to be thanking her. Like everything else, I don't give a flying fuck.

"Was that your way of thanking me?" A smile pulls at her mouth — full of amusement.

"No, it's my way of reminding us both you're mine."

CHAPTER 17

Ellie

On unsteady legs, I open the bathroom door, gathering all my willpower to avoid from reaching out and grabbing hold of the dresser for support, my heart pounding wild from the mere sight of Logan standing in the middle of his bedroom.

Naked.

The second he turns toward me, I take him in. He's holding a piece of paper in his hand, but that's not what drops my jaw.

Appreciation slams into me, jumbling my mind. "Oh my God," I whisper, trying to comprehend how a man can have muscles everywhere that ripple with every movement. This man is solid and vast, and even though I've spent time with him, touched and kissed and gripped. Seeing every inch of Logan blending in with the dim lighting dries my mouth.

My need and nervousness bang around inside my chest. Logan looks like a wild beast. Primal and ready to attack. I follow his free hand, squeezing my thighs together when he wraps it around his hard dick and strokes.

"When I say I want things from you, it's because I need them. When it comes to you, Ellie, those two go hand in hand. Do you understand?" Logan stretches out his hand, giving me the paper. I read it over and sparks fly when I make it to him.

"I understand." God, do I ever. I'm so turned on; I want him to fuck me until I cry.

"You sure, about no protection?"

He grabs my hand, tugging me toward him and kissing my knuckles again before he spins me around. My back to his front, his dick pressing into my ass.

"Yes." I drop the proof from his blood test onto the floor. My fingers shaking and resting limply at my sides.

Logan palms my heavy breasts and growls in my ear. His fingers begin pinching and rolling my nipples and then with a yank, he tears the towel I just wrapped around me after taking a shower clear off my body.

The man leaving me defenseless and completely exposed.

"I want your hands all over me; I need to have mine all over you. I want to suck, bite and mark these tits. I want you wild, and I need you to lose control, Ellie. About lost mine when you stripped out of your bright yellow dress and jumped in the pool. I've been hard for you all day. These braids have my mind thinking about all kinds of dirty. Are you ready to get dirty with me, baby? Remember, I won't ask you to do anything you don't want to do."

Good Lord, this man and his words have my breath hitching at the thought of what he wants and just how filthy we're going to get.

"I'm inexperienced, Logan, not unteachable."

The overwhelming rush of learning and experiencing rushes out of me without an ounce of doubt.

"No one is doing the teaching. We're learning together."

"Then do something already. Make me yours."

"You were mine well before I realized it. The things I want to do to you are nothing short of carnal."

Somehow, I think what he said is mild compared to what he was thinking.

I wiggle my butt provokingly, bumping against his groin and whimper.

A shiver runs through me when he pushes his nose into my hair. His mouth starts moving, placing tiny kisses along the back of my neck — and one hand palms my throat and the other roams down the crack of my ass.

"Spread for me."

I obey, and he plunges his finger inside me, pushing in and out a few times before sliding back up the path it came, circling my puckered hole. I gasp, my head falling back on his shoulder.

Turning me around, Logan kneels at my feet and wraps those big hands around my ankles, skimming upward until he reaches my calves, moving slowly and higher until he touches my core. Cupping it and holding my eyes. Desire nips at my insides, and just like that, I become lost in his touch.

My breath catches when he pushes me onto the bed and pries my thighs apart. Lips finding my skin and drugging me as he works his way up my legs.

"I've never wanted to let someone into my life the way I do you. This thing we have is insane. Take what you learn and feel how good we are together. Me inside you. My cock surrounded by your pussy."

The harsh tone of his words and the heated breath from his mouth accelerate the pulse between my trembling thighs. He pulls away and drags the pad of his thumb across my clit, watching as he does.

"Do you want me to stop?"

"No."

I've been in control of my body for so long. Now, I'm at Logan Mitchell's mercy. A man who is quickly reaching in and taking control of my heart. He's slipping in, digging beneath my foundation, sinking into my soul. It won't be long before he has complete control and I'm falling. I'm not there yet, but I see myself inching closer to the edge — a hard fall. I can only hope he catches me.

His lips part, his tongue darting out to wet his lips, I've wanted that tongue on me everywhere. I've dreamed of it, craved it so many times that I'm going to lose my mind if he doesn't give me what I need.

"Logan, please," I plea.

There's so much desire for this man inside of me that I'm having a hard time breathing while my heart is trying to pound its way out of my chest.

My body presses into the mattress when Logan climbs up my body, placing part of his weight on top of me. His fingers lace through mine. Slowly, he lifts them beside my head. He doesn't say a word. He simply stares at my face.

"I need you inside of me, Logan."

I want more of him. How much more, time will tell. I only know what we've been doing isn't enough. Every time we're together, the air crackles between us.

I swallow when his lips brush across mine, sizzling eyes turn dark as a violent sea after a storm, and yet they don't release my face.

His face is the easiest I've seen it, he swallows hard as he spends a few spellbound moments taking me in.

"Trust me yet? Feel me yet? Doubt yourself?"

The look hidden behind his stare is far from gentlemanly. His darkened gaze makes me want to beg him to kiss me deeply while his hands roam all over the curves of my body. Those eyes of his touch me everywhere, and I like it so, so much that I don't want to break away.

My lips part, my answer releases on a needy pant.

"Somewhat, yes and no."

"Good, then give me the trust you had with your body before you knew who I was. I promise you by the time I'm done feasting and sink my cock into your pussy, you'll be coming hard, heavy, and all over my tongue, fingers, and cock."

He doesn't wait for a reply; he slips down, pulls a nipple into his mouth, and works his magic tongue in a circle. Just when I feel that build between my legs, he moves to the other one. Frustration simmers and rebuilds as he tugs hard, biting and causing pleasurable pain as I've never felt before.

The shameless woman inside me emerges. Never did I think I would know the roughness, the satisfying desire of someone pulling me to the brink of insanity would be something Logan drew out of me as if he's fucked me a thousand times.

"Ready?"

"Yes," Logan swallows, a light layer of sweat breaking across his brows as he pushes off, walks into what I assume is his closet and emerges with two black silk ties.

I swallow, my nerves coming vibrantly alive as he takes my ankles and pulls my legs apart. I gasp, feeling more exposed to this man than I ever have before.

"Logan, you aren't tying my hands too, are you? I'm not ready for you to do that." Panic moves through my lungs as he tugs on my leg, the smoothness of silk weaving loosely around my ankle. I watch, my mind in disarray as he moves to the other and does the same.

Understanding flashes through his eyes. An indication he'd drop his plans in a heartbeat if I asked.

"Just your legs, Ellie. I won't ever restrain all four of your limbs at the same time unless you ask me. I need to be in control, but I need your hands on me. Unless you're on all fours and I'm deciding if I want to fuck your pussy or your ass."

I gasp, my bottom puckering at the thought: mind relaxing and the fear of being tied stops burning in my veins.

"This perfect wet pussy of yours, tight ass, your body, it belongs to me, Ellie, and I'm going to worship you." He slides a finger through my folds, and my back arches, breathing picking up, eyes going wide when he bends, grips his cock and coats the tip with my wetness.

I lift my head when he kneels and pushes a finger into me, muscles squeezing tightly. He dips his head, and the second his tongue meets my clit, I fly upward, fisting the sheets and dropping back down, my head thrashing from side to side. Logan grabs hold of my ass, gathering me beneath him, and licks from the top of my slit to my ass, over and over until my toes curl and my legs are tugging at the restraints to be free.

"Logan, God, please." Once again, I beg, this time not knowing what I'm begging for. Him to bring me to orgasm, to replace his mouth with his cock, to work me into a painful frenzy. All I know is he's driving pleasurable pain straight to the little bundle of nerves I need to set me off.

The growling coming from him mixed with the pulsation through my core as he assaults my tender flesh has me moaning in agony. I scream when he roughly sucks my sensitive clit into his mouth.

Hard.

A massive amount of tingling stimulates me as his tongue impales my body, licking and plunging and attacking like a man possessed — my back arches when his finger curves upward in a deep hard thrust.

In and out, over and over relentlessly while the pressure in my core builds higher and higher, the foreseeable climax starting to work its way from my stomach to between my legs. I scowl, eyes snarling when he stops.

"Foreplay, sweetheart. It can be torture. It'll be worth it when you come so hard all over my face." He lifts his head, a smirk across that mouth dripping with my juices. "Tell me what you need, Ellie."

The knowing grin that stretches over his face sends shivers rippling down my spine.

"You, I need you to finish what you started," I whisper without hesitating. Although, I feel my cheeks heat with embarrassment.

"And then what?"

I shake my head. I knew he wanted control of my body, but it's hard to give him power over my mind when the entirety of it is on edge.

"Then I want you to fuck me, Logan."

He straightens, and I can't take my eyes from the perfect man standing in front of me, viewing me in adoration. "That orgasm you almost had, will be worth the wait when your pussy is weeping all over my cock."

With one hand holding the base of his impressive erection, he drapes over me until his mouth is hovering over my chest, his cock resting at my entrance.

He molds a big hand over one breast and squeezes. His name is rushing out of me on a puff of air when he pinches my nipple, circles the other with the hot tip of his tongue. I nearly explode when he opens his mouth and pulls hard with his teeth.

"You are an enticing temptation — a woman who makes me believe in salvation. The urgency and excitement I feel whenever you are near, a distraction when we're apart. That's how I feel every time I'm with or without you. I can't fucking think straight. You're unraveling me, Ellie Wynn."

His words move through me. The desperation in his voice bearing down on my soul.

I'm burning up. My entire being is on fire.

"I need you inside me, please," I beg. Knowing full well having me do so is what Logan wants.

Surrender.

I'll gladly give it every time we're in bed as long as he gives me what I achingly need.

"Ellie." My name sounds like the beginning of a prayer.

He doesn't give me a chance to catch my breath before he plunges inside me.

And pounds.

My legs burn from being held captive in the restraints; my ass is hanging over the edge of the bed.

I can't move. I can only feel as Logan slams into me.

"Jesus, you feel, God, Ellie, you feel so." His words seem to have escaped him.

"I know." The words are tearing out of my mouth on a gasp. Because I do know, I've known all along that my feelings for him over these past several days has built to something more. Something that's slowly burning. Fervently attacking my mind and scaring the hell out of me.

He grips my waist. Rocks into me with a force that makes my back nearly bend in half, my hips move up and down with his. The headboard is slamming violently into the wall.

He thrust in and out, and I scrape my nails down his back, knowing they'll leave marks.

The way his dick glides in and out of me as I clench and grip him tight is a song to my soul. I feel him everywhere. His heated breath at the base of my neck. His hands as they palm my ass. His dick as it slams into my body at a heart-pounding beat. He doesn't let up with his thrusts as he swirls his hips and takes.

It's a burning desire, a scorching, yearning, craving, beautiful necessity that's been building. The feel of Logan thickening inside of me turns my pants into long, drawn-out moans. Then I hear the faint sound of a groan as his cock starts to pulse.

"Fucking hell." He growls, and my world goes silent, warmth fills me, and my walls grasp hold of him like a hot, flaming sin.

"I wanted you from the minute I saw you," he whispers, his hands whisking up to frame my face. Our noses are touching, our mouths inhaling one another's breaths.

"I'll be right back."

I wince, gathering up the strength to lift my head and admire Logan's backside when he pulls out of me and disappears into the bathroom. My legs burn, my chest growing tight, stomach pitching when he comes back out with a washcloth in his hand.

I pant and given the devilish smirk on Logan's face when he cleans me up, I know he isn't done with me yet.

Life comes back to my legs when he unties them — massaging my ankles and calves before taking hold of my ass, places his knees on the edge and pushes me up the bed.

"Your next orgasm will be in my mouth." His big strong hands squeeze my ass, and he lifts my lower body to meet his face, my legs going around his shoulders.

"Logan." My chest shudders right along with the rest of my body as his lips and tongue zone right in on my clit. Sucking and biting and licking.

"I'm going to come." I can feel that pressure building.

"Not yet." He stops his assault, blows on my sensitive nerve and flicks it repeatedly with his tongue. The man gazing up at me, eyes blown, tongue out of control and going at me like I'm the best thing he's put in his mouth.

I'm thrashing in agonizing pleasure and grinding my pussy boldly into his face.

I moan, closing my eyes in utter bliss as Logan rips another orgasm right out of me.

"One more." It's a demand, not a request.

I'm flipped over on all fours, my braids tugged and fisted in his hand, and I scream so loud, arms barely able to hold me up when he slams into me from behind and fucks me like a madman, deep and hard into my womb.

"Jesus, woman, you feel good."

I scream as he plows into me over and over again, unhinged and out of control. My eyes slam shut, my scalp burns, and I come so hard that static blends with the sound of Logan's skin slapping against mine.

I hear the loud sound of a groan as his cock starts to pulsate, and his strokes become long and slow as he lets go.

I slack onto the bed, shattered, and Logan folds onto me. The heaviness of his body pressing me into the mattress.

I must have blacked out shortly after because when I wake, I'm sore, sated and wrapped up safely in his arms.

CHAPTER 18

Logan

"I'm following someone who was tossed out on her ass. Bitch is sporting some mighty pretty bruises on her face. I told you Ramon doesn't take kindly to betrayal, especially from a bitch who was involved in having someone raped. Any guesses where she's headed? How about who she's with?"

I cringe. Unease settling in my gut.

Grinding my teeth, I press the phone a little tighter to my ear to avoid any chance Ellie might hear Gabe and watch as she bends to place more of the groceries she bought in the refrigerator.

I don't want Ellie hearing about Whitney. That's a subject we haven't broached. Frankly, we haven't talked about her at all since she asked me if I knew where she was.

"Here."

"Yeah. Although I doubt she'll come to your house, not yet anyway. She's with the only friend she has in this town. Am I painting a picture for you yet?"

He sure is, and it isn't like the colorful ones Ellie and Lexi drew the other day that are now all over my fridge.

Not even close.

Motherfucker.

I should have known. Should have seen it coming from a mile away. Should have put two and two together when the now dead fuck told me the woman who hired him to go after Ellie was a blonde.

The thing was, the *she* that's with Whitney never crossed my mind. I guess she's just like her sister, a worthless excuse for a woman. Fuck, this is going to send Lane into a tailspin, and Lexi, I can't even allow myself to think what this could do to her.

Damn it. Why do I have this gut-wrenching feeling things aren't what they seem. That someone close to me is in on this. And there's only one someone it could be.

It hits me all at once, like a bitch-slap to the face, a knife straight to the gut.

I've hardly gotten to know Ellie. In the short time I've spent with her, she's left an impact on me like no other, a ripple effect of vibrant colors, and I knew all along I wouldn't be able to keep her.

Like the fool I said I wasn't, I let go and pretended my life was filled with good when it was mapped out a long time ago to be nothing but a rocky journey to hell.

"I can't take the woman out she's with, son. I can't shoot Whitney until we know what they're up to. We got a sticky problem on our hands."

My skin breaks into a sweat at the same time realization punches me in the chest so damn hard it nearly topples me over.

This is going to end with me hanging on the edge.

A cliffhanger.

One that's jagged and sharp. A shocker to the woman flitting around my house like an angel with wings.

All the things Ellie is doing for me are the most unselfish things any woman has done for me in my life, and here I have women out to ruin me and for what? Money? Influence in a society that's as fucked up as I am?

No woman has cooked me dinner; no woman has spent time with my family. No woman has taken my niece and done girly things. No woman has shown up at my home asking me to help her carry in groceries because she noticed I had little food in my house. And, no woman has laid in bed with me at night asking what my favorite color is, and then two days later I get a delivery from Amazon only to open it and find dishes, silverware, and pots and pans.

Ellie has stamped her imprint all over me.

Fuck. I've gotten myself into a mess.

I have the most remarkable, unforgettable woman taking care of me, and it sends a clusterfuck of images through me thinking there will come a time she'll be doing this with someone else. Someone she deserves. Possibly with kids running around creating havoc and this woman making them her entire world.

Ellie is revitalizing, a life-changer, and not too long ago, I would have played dirty to keep her, but I can't do it if it's going to cause my niece and brother pain.

"Almost finished, oh I nearly forgot, I bought a coffee pot. It's red. You need more color in here, Logan." Ellie whirls around, giving me the most amazing smile I've ever seen before spinning back and bending over again.

Fuck, her ass looks incredible.

I've had that ass up against me every night this week, that tight body crawling all over me with a smile similar when she told me her, Gabe, and Seth were going skeet shooting. I had no idea her dad taught her to play and shoot. That led to her carrying on about Renita teaching her how to cook.

Then again, there's still a lot I don't know about Ellie because I wasted time. Threw her away when all along she should have been mine.

My muscles tick, tightening with need — reinforcing how much I want this woman — falling fast.

I'm going to lose the best thing a man could ask for — a woman who does things out of the kindness of her beautiful heart.

"Do you care where I put it?"

Ellie lifts the coffee pot out of a box, the thing about as bright as her lips. I couldn't give a shit where she puts it. It's her, all her that's bringing color into my world. So gorgeous I want to snag her by the waist and take her where she stands.

Yeah, I'm on a highway to Hell and taking Ellie with me. Goddamn it.

I shake my head, wink, and back out of the kitchen. I sure as hell don't need her to see me this way.

Furious and helpless and hurting. Ever since Ellie came into my life, they've been simmering.

My lungs compress, emotions are now roaring to a boil.

"Sounds like you're over there playing house, building up a dream that might never come true. I told you when you get a taste of good; there isn't anything better. If you want it to have any chance of remaining in the palm of your hands, you need to confess. Last time I'm bringing it up. I support you no matter what you decide because that's what family does, but the longer you don't do Ellie right, the more you disappoint me."

Gabe's words pound a couple more nails into my coffin.

"I have faith in you, Logan. I believe Ellie is falling for you, and you're halfway there. I know hearing that doesn't make it easier. My point, you took some beatings from a woman half your size. Stood there and had men knock you around. You protected your brothers from your mother and those piss-pour excuses for men. On the exterior, you're hard, inside you are just like every other man who falls. It's going to sting like a bitch to tell Ellie, and she may never forgive you. If you want her bad enough, you'll make her understand that all along the things you did were for her."

My conscience pangs against my skull, pressing regret deeper into my brain. Soon, it'll be overflowing with those negative emotions that won't give me a moment's peace. The only time they have were when I was buried so deep in Ellie's tight body all I could think about was how good she felt, how I wanted to keep her forever. How holding her felt right, and talking with her put me at ease.

I'd sensed once I had her again, it would be hard to tell her, grueling in a way I might never get the words out. It'll be my death sentence when she tells me to fuck off.

By no means did I think it would kill me the way it is.

"You make me sound like I asked for this." I let out a chuckle as I fall onto my back on the couch; there isn't an ounce of hilarity to the harsh sound.

"No. You're a man who noticed a young girl years ago and fell before you even knew the right way to make her yours."

"You don't think I know that?" My gut knots up in the knowledge that I'm a coward. I can kill a man, but I can't find it in me to watch a woman fall apart in front of my eyes.

Pathetic.

"Pretty sure you do."

I close my eyes, wishing the words unspoken wouldn't skewer right through my flesh.

Bleeding me dry.

"I should have told her who I was when we talked about the club. She didn't like what I did, but she didn't judge me, she gave me a chance. She gave me a bit of her trust from the get-go. Life might be a hell of a lot easier right now. I told Lane I wanted more. Never did I think at the time I had fallen already. It's only been weeks, Gabe. Fucking weeks and every time I looked at her, those words were on the tip of my tongue — all of them. I didn't have the guts to do it."

I grind my teeth until my gums hurt. I need to feel the pain. Need to feel something but the hope I can someday win Ellie back because my days are numbered. This pretending to play house as Gabe said wasn't a game, it was as real as the woman who set me on a path of righteousness.

"I don't know what to say, Logan. I'll keep my eye on Whitney for tonight. You need to figure out what to do. Talk to Lane because the last person that deserves to be caught up in this mess is Lexi. If it weren't for her, I'd put a bullet in the back of both these bitch's skulls."

Rage pulses and I squeeze my phone. Surprised it isn't shattering in my unsteady hand.

Taking a deep breath, I hang up, toss my phone on the floor beside me and bring my arm to rest across my face. Not sure how long I lay there letting my mind absorb everything. Long enough that when I move my arm, Ellie is standing next to me. A frown has replaced the smile that lit up my kitchen like fireworks.

"Are you okay? You look good there by the way. If you didn't look so tense, I'd think this was the most relaxing side of Logan Mitchell I've seen. Is there anything I can do to help?"

Even with her brows drawn downward, she's so damn pretty. I could stare at her all night and love every second of it. More than likely that's what I'll be doing anyway.

"I'm tired is all, I have a friend in Atlanta who is going through a rough time. He needs me again. Looks like I'm flying out tomorrow."

I'm not flying anywhere, it's Rocco who needs to get his

ass here.

Secrets and lies. So many variations of the vicious pain of betrayal that have been my life. "You don't need to worry about me either. Get down here and give me that mouth."

"You want my mouth? What about what I want?"

Ellie tilts her head, running it slowly down my body, lips parting and tongue sliding out to run across her plump bottom lip when she sees my aching cock straining through my jeans. He's whimpering in agony to be set free.

"You keep that up, and I'm pushing you to your knees."

Fuck, what am I doing?

"Really?" The frown instantly vanishes, replaced with a devious smirk.

"You want my dick in your mouth or are you challenging me?"

She lifts a shoulder, but I see what she's trying to do, the worry in her eyes — the wanting to take whatever is troubling me off my mind.

Son of a bitch, this woman has done run away with my heart. A black one at that.

And here I lay, a prisoner not only to her but also, to a confession filled with regret.

Growing and growing with each passing tick of the clock.

"It's not much of a challenge when I'll drop on my own, Logan."

Desperation hits.

Hard and rash and frantic.

"Drop the clothes willingly too. Those leggings have been driving me crazy hugging your ass since you got here. I want to see how wet you are. I want those tits accessible when you suck my cock until I either come down your throat or fuck you hard right here on this couch. It needs to be broken in. Now strip."

Ellie Wynn lightens my mind, and the mere sight of her

makes me forget the man I am.

I smirk as I sit up and flick open the button of my jeans, lowering my zipper and tugging them down my legs, tossing them off to the side.

This woman is gripping hold of more pieces of me as she obeys and rids herself of her clothes. Dark hair tossed over a shoulder, handfuls of tits and ass in front of me. The perfect pussy is staring me in my face. Not a sign of bashfulness flushes across her smooth skin as she stares at my raging cock.

"Don't think for one minute this is me submitting; it's me getting what I want."

Ellie crosses her arms over her round breasts, pushing those round areolas up, those budded nipples hardening from my greedy stare. My dick twitches against my stomach when she drops to her knees and runs her hands up my thighs.

"That so? It seems to me I'm getting what I want too."

She might be getting ready to blow my mind; I most definitely am not getting what I want.

Her.

"Right. So that you know this is another thing I've never done before."

My pulse starts racing. Ellie is watching me closely, gauging my reaction. What she doesn't see is I suspected as much.

"Makes you all the more perfect to me." How badly I want to tell her no woman has sucked me off without a condom, the same way I've never fucked without one until her. That's a subject sure to sour her mood.

I lift my hand and fist her hair, yanking her toward me and take her mouth while her soft hand grips my throbbing erection — fingertips running across the leaky engorged head.

God, I love the noises she makes when I kiss her. Sexy as fuck and hot as the boiling Louisiana heat. I don't want to leave the warm well of her mouth, but I want it wrapped around me more.

Pulling away, I let her lead.

I jolt, holding back from thrusting upward when the tip of her tongue runs up the length of my shaft.

"Fuck, Ellie." Ecstasy has me throwing my head back, and when she flicks my slit with her sweet little tongue, I find myself shoving my hands in her hair at the same time her mouth slides me inside and sucks.

Flames ignite, a fiery passion roaring through my veins, and spreads right to my balls and the hot center of her mouth.

Desire sweeps away the fear as I watch Ellie work my dick like a pro. Mouth open wide, tongue sliding along my veins, hands working in sync with the bob of her dark head.

"Damn, you keep going at him like that, and I'm going to come. Is that what you want, you want to taste me?" Christ, I hope she does.

"Yes."

Her answer turns into a moan as she takes me to the back of her throat. I lose it then. Both my hands work her head with my slow thrusts.

I prod and drive and groan. She takes it and moans. Giving and loving what she's doing.

"So good, Ellie, fuck, so damn good. Not just this; it's you; all of you." *I'm going to miss you when you're gone. Forgive me. Please forgive me.*

I drop my head to my chest, pinch my eyes closed and fist her hair as I come.

Long into the night after I had her screaming my name as she came in my mouth and around my cock, I knew I was never going to be the same.

CHAPTER 19

Ellie

"You look gorgeous, Ellie. I'm not sorry Logan had to fly to Atlanta and you're stuck with me as your date. That was some of the best food I've had. I am sorry he couldn't see you looking like this though." Norah drains the last of her wine and tosses her napkin on the table.

My hair is wavy and hangs down my back, my makeup is darker than usual, and my white dress dips low, showing off a hint of cleavage. I wanted to dress up for Logan, not that he'd care what I wore. The man has made it clear with actions and words he doesn't expect me to be anything but me. Be that it may, all he's seen me in besides the night we met are jeans and leggings.

"Is that your way of saying I usually look like shit?" I laugh, waving my hand playfully through the air as I finish my glass of wine and push my empty plate forward enough to fold my hands and rest them in front of me.

I've never been into crawfish, but when Logan told me the other night, he wanted to bring me to his favorite restaurant and promised I'd love the crawfish étouffée he wasn't wrong.

"No. It's my way of saying I'm happy for you, Ellie. You're glowing all the time. Logan must be giving it to you good."

My mouth gapes and my attention darts around the restaurant. I lean in, lowering my voice to a whisper and kick her under the table. "I was planning on telling you everything, but our paths haven't crossed much outside of work lately. Now that you've blurted it to all of New Orleans elite, I'm not going to."

It's my fault we haven't seen much of one another. I've been spending my nights with Logan. Some nights we do nothing but talk, others he has me in bed bringing all kinds of pleasure to my body. I find out something new about him every day, and I can't wait to find out more. What we have is fresh and bold. It's crazy and wonderful. Logan Mitchell rescued me.

"I don't need to know the sordid details, the look on your face said it all."

Memories fire through my mind. The man is so big, so dominating, and so good at what he does that he's like an instant high: one hit and my body buzzes. My mind starts racing with the excitement to seek and explore.

I'm relieved that Logan is showing me who he is. I was attracted to him before I realized he's down to earth. I didn't want to be, I wanted to hate him, and I might have if he didn't bulldoze his way through my walls, knocking them down like a man on a mission.

I knew he'd suck me in. Wasn't expecting it to be this quickly. I need to hang on to my heart and trust a little longer though. He hasn't come clean with me about something. Logan will not get all of me until he does.

"His world is frightening, but beneath the hard man is a

romantic and soft guy. He's mysterious, captivating. He's different than I thought he'd be. Dangerous yet safe."

Norah's eyes shift around the room. I know she's thinking of the security who will appear out of nowhere the minute we walk out the door.

It's comforting knowing they are there, still, the idea of anyone having their eyes on me and not knowing what they look like is hard to ignore.

"This isn't me being nosy; it's me being your friend. These past few weeks you and Logan have been caught up in one another. Are you falling in love with him?" A sneaky smile spreads across her face.

She's so full of shit, she smells. I do owe her something though. Logan and I have been living in our own world.

"Falling? Yes. Am I there? Not yet, but it's coming, Norah. I'm scared and excited at the same time," I answer without hesitation.

There are many things I love about Logan. He's playful; he's as much intense as vulnerable. He pushes and pulls; he gives and takes. When Logan looks at me, it's as if he steals every ounce of breath from my lungs. Every time he kisses me, I feel the world tilting. Every time he holds my face in his hands, it feels like he's unraveling all of my knots. Holding me in his muscular arms, I'm growing accustomed to this. For so long, I've longed for it, and now I'm not willing to give it up.

I'm Logan's, and regardless of what he's hiding, Logan is mine.

"I'm happy for you, Ellie. No one deserves to find love as much as you. Let's get out of here."

I start to stand and halt when I catch the eye of a woman heading our way. She strides with purpose, her cruel eyes glaring at me.

She's dressed in a short silver thin strapped dress. It

hangs loosely over her tall model-like frame. Her braless breasts bounce and are practically spilling out of the sides.

The closer she gets, the more her hardened glare directed at me tells me she has a lot to say.

Well, whatever it is, she better be prepared for me to shove it back down her Botox lipped mouth. I might have ignored her at Lexi's party, but that was because I know when and where to keep my mouth shut. I have no qualms about knocking her teeth down her throat if she jerks me the wrong way. Upscale restaurant or not, she'll be knocked down a peg or two.

Trouble making bitches. They can be smelled from miles away.

"Mind if I sit?"

She doesn't wait for me to tell her to march her ass back to where she came from. No, she pulls out a chair, takes a seat and leans toward me. Shoulders squared and elbows off the table. Huge diamond on her wedding finger. How lovely. A married woman who thinks she's going to put me in my place.

What a desperate and pathetic creature she is.

The thought of Logan sleeping with a married woman makes me want to vomit my meal down the front of her. Makes the trust I was finding in Logan slide backward a little too.

I lift a brow in hopes she'll take the hint to get on with it and then get gone before I bitch slap her to the floor.

"Let me be blunt, I have to wonder why a man like Logan would want a woman like you. Are you after his money or do you enjoy the way he fucks you? He's good, isn't he?"

Rage. It just ate up my shock.

"Listen, bitch; I don't know who the hell you think you are—"

"I've got this, Norah," I cut her off. She'll get loud, and this woman might walk away, and I'd like to hear what she has to say.

"You have some nerve coming over here when it sounds to me like you've never gotten the chance to see how good Logan is. Are you jealous Logan is fucking me and not you? Do you have a friend hiding around the corner that sent you over here? Enlighten me please."

I hate her. Hate the idea that Logan might have touched her.

"You don't know the man well enough to know who I am. I have a lot more to say. If you know what's good for you, you'll take your kind and back off."

She's right, I don't and thank God for that. If I had to spend time looking at this woman, I'd carve my eyeballs out.

Steam.

It's billowing off both Norah and me.

"My kind?" I try keeping my voice even, my expression blank, but she turns up a gleaming smirk at me.

Every muscle in my body stiffens. I feel the insult in her icy glare, one that's bouncing right back in her direction, and pegging the bitch between the eyes.

Intimidation doesn't work on me, not after what I've lived through.

"I'm sorry, I didn't catch your name. I'm Ellie Wynn, and this is my friend, Norah. Whatever brought you over here, please get it off your chest, but if you piss my kind off, you'll be sure to know this talk you want to have will end up with you wiping it off the floor right along with your face."

Her eyes go wide with the deliberate slip of my tongue.

"Let me rephrase. Do you have any idea who Logan is?"

My blood boils as she sits in front of me all smug and proper. Eyes are searching for a sign of weakness. She won't find one. Knowing when to hold and release is another thing I've learned well.

I dig my nails into my palms as I try to calm myself. Violence and I don't get along, but this woman is making me question just how good it would feel to thump her off the chair and I will without giving it a second thought.

"I know who he was, and my guess is you'd like to steer me clear of him. Are you here to speak for a friend, for yourself or for all of you who aren't good enough to hold Logan's attention?"

There is no stopping the tremor of discomfort that slides down my spine. My brain is struggling to understand why this phony woman seems to think she needs to warn me. I shove the thought of Logan being intimate with this woman away. I do care about the women he's slept with before me, but not in the way she's hoping. I care because it was one of them who sent someone after me. It could easily have been her. Makes me wonder how many more are going to crawl out of the woodwork and come at me.

I'm not about to bring it up. I might not trust Logan completely, but I do trust it won't be long until he finds out who it was. And I believe him when he said he hasn't been with anyone since we met. Makes me curious as to why she's here.

I lean forward, hiding the fear she might tell me something that will crush me. I cover it with anger and hope she picks up the scent coming out of every pore in my body.

She stiffens.

"I didn't come over to argue with you. I came to warn you. It's your choice if you want it or not."

She's lying.

My body pulsates with a compelling forcefulness to lunge across the table and strangle her. I never knew I had this much pent up anger in me. It's a laughing shock to my system. I squeeze my lungs to hold it in. To not dig her judgmental eyeballs out of their sockets that are looking at my dress as if I'd picked it out of a garbage can.

"I don't. So Logan has a past. All of us do. Unlike you, appearances mean nothing to me, but Logan does, and I will not let you warn me away. It was you, wasn't it? You sent someone to hurt me and you didn't do it for yourself, did you?"

The woman studies me. Lips are curling as she drags her gaze up and down my body. Once again, I feel disappointment crashing over me, little pins and needles poking at my skin, trying to puncture through in hopes of drugging me with a reminder that I'm not meant to be in Logan's world. But I won't let her take that away from me. Logan has spent the better part of our time together proving he isn't the typical millionaire. He's a lot like my father. He is giving and caring of his time. Loves his family fiercely and the way he is with Lexi makes the man sexier than anything else.

Regardless of what he's hiding from me, he makes me feel special and wanted, and no matter what Logan told me about him not being a good man, he is with me, and this woman can take her warning and shove it right up her ass.

"You might know parts of Logan, but you don't know them all. He isn't at all who you think. He's calculating, cunning, and he is hiding something big from you. If you don't believe me, go to his house and check it out for yourself."

"Get up, you filthy fucking bitch. How could you do this? Go home and wait for Logan, Ellie. Norah, don't you dare leave her alone. I promise this woman will never bother the two of you again."

I jolt at the dark figure leaning over the table. Muscles in his face twitching, hands balling into fists and his upper body moving slowly to crowd this woman's space. Shock rocks me back in my chair from what she said. More worriedly, it's what Lane said as he stares her down with so much hatred she flinches.

Somehow I believe the only one speaking the truth here is her.

CHAPTER 20

Logan

"Where are you, Ellie?" I drop my phone on the floor next to me and bow my head, barking out a grunt of disgust as I do.

It's ironic, how I'm on my knees when that's what I told Ellie I wanted from her.

I slam my eyes closed. Wrath sweltering in my blood. Simmering rage that blisters at my guts.

Revulsion and agony and a pang of guilt busting me open.

All of me spinning.

I hate this city. Hate every damn thing about it. It's offbeat, loud, and proud. It's made up of more cultures uniquely their own. And even though it's below sea level, it's resting on a swamp of scavengers.

The Big Easy, they say. It's easy, alright. Easy to get lost in a world that screws with people's minds.

It's the city of colorful sex from Bourbon Street to the Bayou. It's a pleasurable activity in which any willing person can learn and participate. But it also can come with a price if you're the master and those you fuck take what you give them and turn it into something ugly.

At the moment, I'm not sure which I hate more, this city, myself, or the choices I made.

That's the thing about choices; you can never go back and erase them. Never undo what's done.

There were many times I kept wondering the same thing over again. Kept berating myself, always asking why I'd take apart my life a piece at a time. Never got an answer. Suppose that's par for the course when you've lived a life trying to protect someone and get back what was rightfully theirs when all along, all I'd had to do was knock on Ellie Wynn's door.

But no. I had to twist the knife. Had to make someone pay. A lot of fucking good it did when it's about to destroy.

I can't imagine what would've happened years ago if I would've gone to Ellie instead of seeking out revenge. Maybe it would've been the only push I needed to claim what's mine. But this is my torment. My hell on earth. My old goddamn fault.

Torturer.

Sinner.

The deceiver who feels the gaping hole of losing the best thing that happened in my life in my chest, it nearly caves thinking about what Ellie knows and where she is.

Karma and fate.

They make a deadly combination, both coming into my life at the same time.

The first is a cold-hearted slap to the face.

The second I never believed in, not until I saw Ellie perched up on a bar stool looking like some kind of wet dream. Her laugh contagious. Her innocent eyes searching for something only someone seeking out the same would find.

To be needed.

To be loved.

Yeah, karma. She's always the one who twists up fate.

Crushing it beneath her heeled boot.

What a fucking cunt she is.

There is much more at stake in this deadly game than losing Ellie.

Lexi and Lane will be hurt in irreparable ways if I don't play my hand right.

I've derailed Ellie's life, and I'll live with it, but disrupting the life of an innocent little girl who could be dragged through hell, I'd rather be shoved back through the burning gates.

Ever since I can remember, I've always protected my brothers. I didn't do it because I was the oldest and felt it was my duty. I did it out of love, and regardless of how fucked up our lives are, how deep into guilt Seth is, how shallow the well is that makes up the life Lane worries about day and night. I'll protect them for the rest of my life.

There were times when our dad would tell me to let them fight their own battles with the neighborhood kids. He'd say "Son, your intentions are good, I get why you don't want anyone to hurt your brothers, and there's nothing wrong with it, but you protect a little too fiercely."

I didn't listen to him then, wouldn't if he were still alive. Tonight is one of those nights where Lane has to protect himself from a woman who done lost her mind; it'll be my fault if things don't go his way.

Should have said fuck it all and had Gabe end the woman who must have approached Ellie because she found out some of the things I've done.

Mainly? Murder.

I was almost done digging someone's grave when my

phone kept repeatedly vibrating in my back pocket. I answered when I saw it was Lane.

I made him aware this morning. Told him to stay out of it and to keep Lexi by his side. He didn't listen. He dropped Lexi off with Gabe, searched all over town for the woman who is out for his blood, and when he found her, it was too late. She'd approached Ellie.

Lane made her leave, and when he walked her to her car, she laughed in his face when he asked what she told Ellie. Frustrated and angry, I'm sure when he knew he wouldn't get anywhere.

Lexi's aunt, Sadie Ferguson. Her mother's sister is the one who hired someone to hurt Ellie. Also, the one who picked up Whitney from Ramon's. She's a conniving woman just like her sister who walked out of the hospital after giving birth to Lexi before her discharge papers were even dry.

Stephanie, Lexi's mom, not once held that precious baby. She blindsided my brother and left Lexi without a mother. Better off, but it left Lane filled with worry about when the day comes where Lexi starts asking about her mom, the repercussions of abandonment it could have on that little girl's mind.

I've told him dozens of times he's the best father I know, and he'll figure it out the same way he's managed to raise her on his own, but I don't walk in his shoes. I don't tuck that angel in bed every night. Don't sit around wondering if it's Stephanie every time someone knocks on my door.

And now, I sit here waiting on Lane's call before I make my next move.

"There you are. Your security is gone. Were you expecting me or were you hoping your little bitch might show up? Me, I was looking forward to the latter."

My head kicks up, and I shoot Whitney right between the eyes with my frosty glare.

She's a dead bitch for double-crossing me.

"You bought furniture, or did Ellie buy it for you? We have many topics to discuss, Logan. There's Lexi; there's Maggie, Stephanie and Sadie, and Ellie. Oh, more importantly, there's me. Which one would you like to chat about first?"

Whitney sends me one of those twisted smiles I've seen plenty of times over the years as she waltzes in and kneels in front of me, her short skirt riding up her thighs. The bitch wants more from me than talk; she wants something she isn't ever going to get again.

My cock and my safety.

I rough a hand down my face, trying to stay calm.

"What did you do to Maggie, darling. Did you kill her yourself? God, you're tense. Do you need me to help you out with that?" She rubs her hands up my thighs.

Nausea whirls. My hands shoot out and I grip her by the throat.

A riot starts in my body. Fighting and dueling in my skull. The reminder of what I was, what Whitney and I used to do and what could have been if she wouldn't have done what she did.

Christ, I can't even imagine it. Being with this bitch, thinking she was my world once upon a time.

Need.

It trumps and squashes.

This woman or any other isn't what I need. Not by a long shot. Replaceable. They all are.

Ellie is not.

"You'll never know what I did, you're good as fucking dead." I know better than to confess to Whitney about killing someone. I haven't trusted her since I found out she conspired with Shadow.

Maggie is out of the picture. She was someone I trusted

with everything, and she betrayed me. She might have been a possessive one, but I never thought she'd be this desperate to have me, and by doing so, she'd fed Whitney information about Ellie. It wasn't until Rocco and I went to see Maggie that she confessed while I put a gun to her head. She's the one who let Whitney into the club and handed over my laptop. She's the one who did a lot of things, and she's no longer breathing.

Bitch was like all the rest of the women who want me. Not one of them looks at me like they'd run off into the sunset with me with nothing but a pot to piss in. Not one of them can stand on their own two feet like Ellie. They don't feel like her, taste like her. Dress like her. They aren't *her*.

Even the one in front of me. A woman I once loved. A woman I pretended to still care about long after her brother went to jail, and now she's here to try and stake her claim.

To fuck Ellie all over again.

Because of me.

Right.

That'll never happen. Not while I'm breathing.

"What the hell did Sadie say to Ellie?"

"She tried warning her, and you know why?" Tilting her head to the side, she pins me with a glare. Deep satisfaction is written all over her face. "Tell Lane to let Stephanie and Sadie see Lexi. Give me back what you took from me and I'll prepare you for when you see Ellie next. I'll see to it she forgives you."

She may as well have kicked me in the balls. My entire body winds tightly with worry.

But I mask it the same way I've done for years with Whitney. She might be good at manipulation, I'm a hundred times better. Only problem? I won't jeopardize my niece. I can't do a damn thing until I hear from Lane.

"Lane will never agree to that. I'm not playing around

with you anymore. Told you that years ago when I found out you were the one who snitched on Shadow. Guess my proof will be in your brother's hands by tomorrow." I squeeze tighter, crawling up her skanky body until I'm in her face.

Cold laughter pours out of her mouth, covering her with the poisonous woman she is. "I'd think twice before you start throwing demands my way."

Bitch doesn't have a leg to stand on with me.

"And I'd start thinking about just how much you want to live if I were you."

My head spins and my heart pounds, bile climbing up my throat, revulsion crawling across my flesh.

"What I took from you wasn't yours to begin with, Whitney. You should know better than to try and get a dime from me."

"I'm here to do what should have been done a long time ago. Make you pay, Logan. I have the upper hand this time. I have proof to get Lexi taken from her daddy. I have proof to make Ellie run. I have proof, you have nothing."

I breathe deeply to settle the fuming pulsation of my muscles, the wrath boiling through the thick layers of my skin ready to hit my veins and burst open any minute.

Misery.

It bounds me tight.

"Where's my laptop?"

My head spins and my heart pounds, bile climbing up my throat, revulsion crawling across my flesh.

My blood boils as Whitney licks her lips, relaxed in her pose, gratification pouring out of her.

"Give me what I want, Logan, and I'll tell you. The quicker you do, the faster you can beg Ellie to forgive you. Although, I'm not sure anymore if she will."

Dread rocks through my veins as Whitney's eyes shift to my front door.

I can feel Ellie's life-force drain away in my doorway, screaming for a breath, for some air before she speaks.

"Oh, God. No. Have you been fucking her the whole time you've been with me? What do I need to forgive you for, Logan? I would have forgiven you for anything, but her."

My stare rips from Whitney to Ellie. The woman so beautiful I can't bear to see the tears falling down her face, the wringing of her hands. The shock of her seeing Whitney in my house, and me on top of her.

Sickening, cynical laughter breaks from Whitney's all too happy mouth. I can feel her claws digging in.

A vicious circle of deceit. Round and round it goes.

"Oh, this is better than I thought it would be. You should have learned your lesson years ago not to mess with me, Ellie. Funny thing how I've lived in this town for years and never knew you did too. Not until a few weeks ago. We could have shared Logan the way I shared him with everyone else. We could have bonded like sisters again. I wish I could say it's nice to see you again, but it's not. I'm sorry to be the one to tell you this. I'm Logan's wife, and we're having a baby. I'm four months along."

ABOUT THE AUTHOR

USA Today Best Selling Author Kathy Coopmans is a Michigan native where she lives with her husband, Tony. They have two son's Aaron and Shane.

She is a sports nut. Her favorite sports include NASCAR, Baseball, and Football.

She has recently retired from her day job to become a full-time writer.

She has always been an avid reader and at the young age of 50 decided she wanted to write. She claims she can do several things at once and still stay on task. Her favorite quote is "I got this."

Release notifications- text Kcoop to 21000